BUTCHER'S
Babygirl

SIOBHAN SMILE

Hostile
WHISPERS PRESS

BUTCHER'S BABYGIRL

SIOBHAN SMILE

HOSTILE WHISPERS PRESS, LLC

BUTCHER'S BABYGIRL

AUTHOR NOTE

Toni

At thirty-three, I was hopelessly in love with my best friend and roommate, Aisling Butcher. She was everything I wanted but could never have because I wouldn't break that barrier. My fear of losing her was too much to transcend. That didn't mean I didn't live for every adoring expression when she looked at me. Yet how much longer could I remain strong before I revealed my secret?

Butcher

My baby sister's best friend, Toni, was flawless. She was everything I'd always wanted but knew I couldn't possess. She was always my Babygirl. Her happiness and safety my only concern in life. That's why I wouldn't make my feelings known. I wasn't good enough. I wouldn't let my demons touch her perfection. But when teasing kisses turn to more, am I brave enough to claim what's mine?

(CW: Past sexual abuse. Homophobia. Addiction. If these subject matters are triggering to you, please feel free not to read. Readers, your mental and emotional safety is important, and self-care should take precedence. Thank you.)

Copyright © 2021 by Siobhan Smile & J.M. Dabney

Hostile Whispers Press, LLC

ISBN: 978-1-947184-50-3

Print ISBN: 978-1-947184-51-0

Cover by: Hostile Whispers Designs (J.M. Dabney)

Formatting by: Hostile Whispers Designs (J.M. Dabney)

Editing by: Jessica Montgomery

REMEMBER:

This book is a work of fiction. All characters, places, and events are from the author's imagination and should not be confused with fact. Any resemblance to persons, living or dead, events or places, is purely coincidental.

PLEASE BE ADVISED:

This book contains material that is only suitable for mature readers. It may contain scenes of a sexual nature and/or violence.

PROLOGUE

TONI

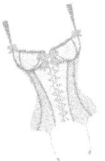

Fall 2005

ANOTHER WEEK DOWN IN THE DRAMA THAT WAS HIGH school, and my best friend, Fern, and I were waiting outside for her sister to arrive. Aisling Butcher had been my secret obsession since I hit puberty, but she'd been an out and proud lesbian forever. Fern and I were lifelong friends since we met on the first day of kindergarten. Aisling was the older sibling who had never really wanted us hanging out too much, especially when she'd started high school. She was better now that we were older, but not by much.

We'd formed a bit of a truce when I came out as bisexual the previous year. She'd given me and Fern a safe space in her crappy off-campus apartment. As much as I loved my parents, they weren't understanding, so I hid securely in the closet outside Fern and Aisling. When I'd come out as a transgender girl a few months earlier, I'd waited for my friends not to be as cool about it. That hadn't happened, and surprisingly Aisling let us hang out more and more.

"What's going on?" I asked.

"I don't know. Aisling said she was picking us up and to wait. You know she only does what she wants. And god forbid someone tells her no."

Most people thought Aisling was an asshole, and she was, but it was about her not giving a shit about what people thought of her or what she did with her life. She was going to college with plans to join the police academy afterward. She'd already had her life planned out. I loved how self-assured she was, and I was jealous I couldn't be me until I turned eighteen. Transitioning would have to wait until I moved out of my parents' home.

I still had doubts if I was doing or feeling the right way. I still wore my *boy* clothes. I shaved in the hope the peach fuzz covering my face would thicken and make me look less androgynous. I worked to keep my voice deep. Fern and I pretended to be more than friends. I hated looking at myself in the mirror and not seeing the me I knew I was. The realization something wasn't right was when Fern started her period, had to buy her first bra, and her hips got wider, and I was envious.

A horn beeped, and we looked in the direction to find Aisling's car idling in the pickup lane. We rushed to get in. Fern hopped in the back, and I rode up front.

"What's the big secret?" Fern demanded an answer as soon as we pulled toward the exit.

"You two can wait."

Aisling had her hair pulled back in a tight ponytail. She played rugby every weekend with a bunch of her friends and worked out with them several times a week, so she was more muscular than the girls I knew. Her t-shirt showed off her thick bicep as she rested her wrist on the top of the steering wheel, and she slightly slouched in the seat. She had this confidence that you didn't see in a lot of nineteen-year-olds. I think that had a lot to do with the open and honest relationship she had with her parents. Nothing was off-limits for conversation in her family. Anyone could discuss anything without fear of rejection.

That security wasn't present in mine to that degree. My dad and I had a great relationship, we spent hours at his garage talking, and he was always affectionate. He'd told me about his dad being emotionally unavailable, which he'd said was pretty much standard for that generation. But he wanted to make sure I never thought emotions were bad things. My mother was the opposite. She was strict, and her Church was everything. "God is good all the time" was her favorite line, and she said if we lived by the Lord's word, then He would take care of us. I didn't know if I believed as deeply or easily as she did, but Church wasn't an option, so I went when she told me to go.

I darted a glance at Aisling just in time to find her looking at me as we waited at a red light.

"You have to be home a certain time?" she asked as she pushed the gas pedal.

"No, Mom has her women's group, and Dad has to work late. So, the usual curfew."

"I'll get you home in plenty of time."

When we reached her apartment, she pulled into a spot in front of her building. The place was falling apart and mostly housed college students. There were always the lingering scents of weed and cigarette smoke, and when the sun went down, a lot of parties broke out. I never let my parents know when I went to her place. They wouldn't approve of their teenager hanging out with college kids.

"Come on, we'll take care of what we need to do, and then I'll order pizza or Chinese before I get y'all home." The driver's door creaked as if it were about to fall off the hinges.

I shot a glance at Fern, who still looked confused, but we followed anyway. Aisling waved and talked to a few people she seemed to know. She turned down the invitation to smoke or come in for a beer. When a few of the guys checked out Fern, she made sure they backed off her *sixteen-year-old* sister. She had this husky voice that deepened slightly when she was pissed.

We took the stairs to the fourth floor and huddled around her as she unlocked her apartment door. I knew she worked odd jobs, even worked as a bouncer at some clubs. Her parents had tried to pay for everything. She'd refused and said she'd make her own way. I liked that about her, too—her independence.

The interior was dark. There was the scent of Nag Champa incense in the air. She jiggled her key out of the lock, and we entered. I was still unsure of why she was being so secretive. The lights turned on, and there was a pile of wrapped presents on the table, in the hottest pink I'd ever seen outside of neon. They looked so out of place in the apartment and its thrift store furniture. It wasn't Fern's birthday. That had happened months before.

"So, what are we doing here? You're being weirder than normal."

Aisling glared at Fern, and for the first time, Aisling spread her hand along my lower back. She led me to the coffee table. "Go ahead. They're all yours." She didn't say anything else as she flopped into a recliner listing dangerously to the side.

I turned to Fern, and she shrugged her shoulders and walked around to the couch to sit down. I tossed my backpack to the floor and reached for the first box. It was about shirt-sized, and I carefully ripped the paper. I felt Aisling's full attention on me. Yet, I forced myself not to look at her. I tried never to focus on her because I feared she'd see my interest. That would be embarrassing.

My body went strangely a mixture of hot and cold as I removed the top of the box, and in wrinkled white tissue paper rested a pretty, yellow sundress, and I dropped everything but the dress. I held the too-soft cotton in my left hand as I shot a glance at Aisling. She was smiling, full-on with lips and eyes.

"What—" My voice broke, and I darted my gaze to find Fern as shocked as me.

"I know you can't be you at home, but here, in my shitty place, you can be. I got you other stuff." She motioned with her hands for me to open the rest, but I didn't want to put the dress down.

I opened present after present, and a pile of makeup, silicone breast inserts, panties, bra, and even a pair of shoes formed. The more I looked, the more I felt the tears rolling down my cheeks.

"Go on, try everything on and then come out and let us see."

I didn't know what to say. "Thank you" didn't seem to hold enough weight. I gathered up everything but the makeup, rushed to her bedroom, and locked myself inside. Voices were muffled on the other side. With shaking hands, I stripped away my clothes and put on the items she bought me. There was no mirror in her bedroom for me to take in my appearance.

I fought with my fear and exhilaration. I'd never dreamed of anything like this. It was a reality in the distant future when I could be free, and I'd found my place in the world. My hand shook on the doorknob, and it took me several times to open it.

When I stepped out, Fern was staring at me with even more tears, and Aisling had her back to me as she placed a full-length mirror in a corner that I'd never seen before. She turned to the side, and she still had the smile, the one that said she was happy for me. I couldn't understand why she did it. None of the stuff she bought me could've been cheap, and she was a broke college student.

"Did I get the fit right?"

I couldn't answer, just nodded. The items, even the bra, seemed to be made for me, and my bare feet sunk into the cheap, ugly carpet, but at that moment, the rundown apartment was like a mansion. Aisling held out her hand, and I took it. I purposely avoided my reflection and instead kept my eyes on her but then let them close.

"Come on, babygirl. Look how beautiful you are." She moved behind me with her hands on my hips and positioned me in front of the mirror. I almost protested when she moved away. "Take your time. We're in no rush."

I heard the creaking of the recliner. I kept my breaths deep and even. My secret wish would be revealed as soon as I opened my eyes and looked at myself. I inhaled for a count of eight, and as I exhaled, I opened my eyes to take in the stranger staring back at me.

The yellow of the dress was so startling and beautiful against my dark, brown skin. The top of it flowed over the falsie stuffed cups, and the full flowing skirt gave the impression of hips. Sobs broke through my fight to contain them.

"Isn't she beautiful, sis?" Aisling asked, and I caught her staring at me in the mirror. There was something soft and strange about her expression. She had her elbow rested on the arm of the chair, and her chin rested on her upraised hand.

That was the moment I knew I was in love with Aisling Butcher and always would be.

1

BUTCHER

Sixteen Years Later

THE LOUD POUNDING ON MY BEDROOM DOOR WOKE ME UP, and I frowned as I pushed the slender arm off my chest. I threw my legs over the edge of my bed and pushed up, stumbling to the door in nothing but my boxer briefs. I knew who waited on the other side, and she'd seen me naked more times than I could count in our years as friends and roommates. Throwing open the door, my sister's best friend Toni stood there glaring at me. She as a goddess; sexy and perfect and her simple presence tortured me every day .

"Good morning, babygirl." I smirked at her massive eye roll.

"What did I tell you about bringing women home, Butcher?"

"Gag them?"

"Exactly." She stormed off down the hall with her bright bonnet covering her hair and robe still on.

"What the hell time is it?"

"Five a.m. If I can't sleep, you're not sleeping."

"Aw, baby, you know you love me." I chuckled as she flipped me off over her shoulder. "Make coffee."

I went back to the bed and the nameless woman on it. Did we even exchange names? I shrugged as I shook the woman awake.

"Time for you to go, my babygirl is home and pissed."

She went from smiling sleepily and probably thinking about round three to panicked and running like her ass was on fire. I heard a squeak outside the door and shot a glance over my shoulder as I pulled on my binder to find Toni glaring at me. I'd taken a shower to get rid of the woman's perfume from my skin after she'd passed out.

"Was that necessary?"

I adjusted my binder until my breasts were comfortable inside it and then turned.

"Half asleep, my girl home and pissed, less chance I have to give her my number."

"Are you ever going to find a woman you like?"

"I like you."

"You know what I mean. You can't keep going out to bars every night to pick up some stranger." She exited my room, and I followed; she wasn't done bitching at me. "This hyper-sexed unfeeling-stud thing you got going on isn't attractive."

Wouldn't she love to know my bed partners were fewer and farther between the last five years since she'd moved in with me the last time? Most nights I was at the bar, it was with the guys I worked with. A woman had needs and not being able to have the one you wanted, well, you did what you had to do. Toni wanted her happily ever after, find her Prince or Princess Charming. Since high school, she wouldn't get into a relationship with someone if she didn't see it going somewhere, and the first time they asked for sex before she was ready, she shut them down. That's why she and my sister had the arrangement in high school to pretend to be a couple.

I couldn't be that person for her, and I knew it. Not that I couldn't be monogamous or committed. She hated my job; she worried constantly about my safety. The fact I may act like I had a death wish didn't help. I'd spent seven years as a cop and had some major authority issues, so I'd signed on with a friend who had a Bail Bond Business, and I had the background and craziness he needed. Wasn't saying much for my mental state.

"Babygirl, I work hard. I go out and find some woman to bring home. What's the big deal?"

"You're getting too old to act like you're invincible."

"Ouch." I took the heavy mug of coffee she handed me. "I'm only thirty-six."

She glanced over her shoulder and let her gaze rake my exposed skin. I knew she stopped on every scar—especially the ones on my left shoulder that almost destroyed it. The guy had used a shotgun at a distance, and the force of the shot wasn't as bad as it could've been. They'd mostly had to dig out the pellets, and I had doctor-ordered physical therapy. She'd rode my ass for two months and didn't talk to me for a week when I went back to work without clearing it with my doctor.

"But bullets and blades love you. What about that guy who tried to take you out with his SUV?"

"We've talked about this. My job is dangerous, but it's not always like that. You just blow up the injuries."

"Oh, I blew up that time you nearly lost a kidney?"

"But I didn't."

"You're impossible, and I don't know why I talk to you." She tried to storm past me, and I grabbed her arm as I set my mug aside.

I spun her until I could wrap my arms around her slender waist to keep her there. She was only a few inches taller than my five-nine, but I was stocky and built to fight. She was slender and no match for me. Not that she was pulling away. We'd been in each other's personal space too many times. I knew most people believed we'd been a couple for years, but I wasn't that fucking lucky.

"Toni, I promised to come home every night if possible, didn't I? How many times have I broken that promise?"

"Too many. I have to get ready for work."

I let her go and leaned back against the counter. She'd been my sister's best friend, three years younger than me. I'd spent high school and college driving them around while they did all those things I rolled my eyes over, but I always liked making Toni happy. Like when I bought her her first dress and makeup when she'd confessed to Fern and me that she was transgender. We'd kept her secret until she was eighteen and away at college.

Her family had taken it hard, did the whole bullshit mourning thing families sometimes do. Her mom had disowned her, but her dad had come to the school or met her in town or at my apartment to spend time with her. When she wasn't living with me my home became hers on breaks and summer vacations.

We'd lived together one way or another since she was nineteen and then five years previously things fell through at her old place when her roommate found a boyfriend. He hadn't wanted Toni around, and what had I done? I'd taken my truck and packed her and her things into it and brought her home.

I'd always loved her, first as a friend, and then something changed over the years as she transitioned and became herself. She'd become lighter and happier. That hint of sadness that clung to her disappeared. I'd fallen in love with Toni and realized how fucked I was.

She didn't like I was a player. She didn't like my job. She thought I was still living in my twenties and felt I needed to grow up and do big girl things. Aisling Butcher was not the woman for her. She'd made that plenty clear. Not outright, but her wants and needs were as far from me as they could get.

She had a list of requirements, and she never deviated from

it. I always joked she was too picky. Yet part of me was happy no one would ever live up to her standards, and I knew that made me an asshole. I was honest about it, though. The only thing I'd never been honest about was the fact that I wanted her for mine.

Even if I confessed, I doubted she'd agree or believe me. I hadn't exactly made myself appealing. I picked up my mug and chugged the tepid coffee and put it in the sink. I didn't have to be at work until ten, maybe a power nap and then another shower after I changed my sheets to get rid of the stranger's presence.

I strode back to my room and heard the shower running where she'd left her bedroom door cracked. When I entered my room, I remove my binder and fell face-first into bed. I just needed more sleep, and then I'd be back to normal, or as normal as I get.

2

TONI

"WHAT DID BUTCHER DO NOW?"

At Fern's question, I jerked my head up and realized I'd been staring at my salad; I hadn't even touched it yet. "What do you mean?" We both worked in jobs close to each other; we had a standing lunch date unless something came up. I should've canceled because I knew my oldest friend would notice I was off, and I just wasn't in the mood to talk about Butcher.

"Come on, Toni. When my sister does something that bothers you, you get all weird."

"She's just Butcher." And that was true. She'd come out of the closet the moment she was born. She'd always been loud and proud and dared anyone to say anything. That had been one of the reasons I'd felt so comfortable telling them I was bisexual and then trans in high school. It was two years of personal revelations, and they accepted me so easily I'd felt like a bitch for doubting them.

I remembered the exact moment I'd fallen in love for the first and last time. She'd picked Fern and me up from school one afternoon and taken us to her apartment. She'd been in her sophomore year of college.

I'd walked in to find a pile of hot pink paper-wrapped presents. The smile on her face when I'd come out of her bedroom had been almost as big as mine after the shock wore off, and I truly looked at myself in the mirror. We'd spent the afternoon at her place, and Fern had done my makeup. Her apartment became my safe place where I kept all my dresses and makeup, my address for everything I ordered with her bank card. I always gave her the money, but I lived two years of freedom in her tiny rundown apartment. Where I was always she and her, I was me.

The day it happened, I was so shocked it hadn't fully hit me until I'd gotten home and I realized what she'd done for me. She'd instinctively known exactly what I needed before I had even figured it out.

"Earth to Toni. Another one-night stand?"

I shook my head to clear it of memories. "When aren't they one-night stands?" I started eating and hoped it covered my irritation. The women she brought home or flirted with when we went out never looked like me. Her type always petite with big breasts and adorable.

"You know you two act like an old married couple."

"That's bullshit. You know I just worry about her and her lack of caution."

"I worry about her, too, yet I know she's not going to change. She's been the same her entire life, but she loves you. And she tries to make you comfortable. How many times a day does she call or check in when she's working or off on a job?"

"That's not the point. I can't check on her. I adore you, Fern, but she's been a huge part of my life since I was sixteen. We've lived together. It's just she has a fucking death wish."

Fern waved her hands. "Off the complicated discussion of my adrenaline junkie sister, there's a new guy at work."

"No, I'm still not recovered from the last date with the TERF (trans-exclusionary radical feminist) lesbian." I grinned at her frustrated growl. I forgot how many times she'd apologized for that one.

"She seemed so fucking cool, and I had no damned idea. I mean, what the fuck does it matter your genitals? I mean, come on. She still walks a wide circle around me at work. I think that might have more to do with her picking you up and Butcher answering the door in her vest, badge, and weapon. I think she did that on purpose, though. My sister is a little scary."

Little? Butcher was almost five-ten with muscles but not overdone. Still cuddly, but I'd never say that aloud. I'd seen men twice her size back down with just a look from her.

"Okay, for real, no more talk of Butcher. Okay, Aaron is very nice. Bisexual. He's been single for a year since he broke up with his boyfriend. I told him about you, and he's interested in a date. It's a meal and conversation. What could it hurt? Should I give him your number?"

"Sure, why not. I can't remember the last time I went out on a date."

"Great, I'll give it to him when I see him this afternoon. Did mom and dad call you?"

"Mom did. She was making sure I wasn't missing Sunday dinner and made me promise to bring Butcher."

"That's been weird. She's been avoiding the parents for the last year for some reason. Except for holidays, she's always telling them she's working, but I know that's not true because I have my in-house spy."

I finished off my food, picked up my iced tea, and leaned back in my chair. "She's been kinda weird overall the past year. A lot more time at work."

"How's her drinking?"

I suppressed my groan at the question. The conversation happened far too often. Fern and her parents brought it up every few months. While I hated the women she brought home from the bars, she never smelled of alcohol or looked hungover.

Butcher had the shortest temper when she was drinking. Not that she didn't have some anger issues when she was sober, but she'd never taken it out on her family or me. Usually, she reserved that for her punching bag in the garage or the gym where she trained.

"She flips her new two years sober coin between her fingers when she's thinking too much. As far as I know, she's still going to her meetings."

Those three years where she'd seemed to lose herself for some reason still haunted me. I knew she'd probably done more than drink, but she never talked about it or why it happened. One night she'd come home from work, and she'd been normal, and then the next, she'd disappeared for two days. I'd done everything to find her. I'd worried myself into a rage until her parents brought her home. She'd looked like hell. From that day forward, she wasn't the same.

Since she'd started her meetings, some of the spark was back but not as much as before.

"Okay, I have to get back to work." I stood, and she did the same. She hugged me, and we kissed each other's cheeks. We split our bill.

On the way back to my building which was a short walk away, my thoughts went to Butcher. My feelings were confused when it came to her. While I loved her, she didn't fit my list. Part of me thought that's why I made the list. If I stuck to it, then I could justify ignoring my feelings for her.

I didn't want to lose my second family, the one who'd made me safe and comfortable in the beginning when I was losing my mind. Who'd lessened my worry over losing everything when I came out. If I gave in and it didn't work out, I couldn't live without Butcher. We'd been friends and roommates for more than half my life. She'd leave a huge hole, and I couldn't chance that.

As I stepped out of the elevator on my floor, my phone rang, and I pulled it out of my pocket.

"Hello?"

"Hey, babygirl. How's your day?"

Male voices murmured in the background, which meant she was at the office.

"Good, I just had lunch with Fern." I entered my office and closed the door behind me. I opened the bottom drawer of my desk to stow my purse.

"Did you tell her I was still sober?"

"Of course. Your family just worries. You don't gotta use that tone." I could picture her massive eyeroll.

"I know they worry. Speaking of worry, I won't be home tonight, probably not until tomorrow evening. We've got a stakeout at this dude's old lady's house to see if he shows up."

"Make sure you eat something other than greasy fast food and drink more than coffee." I laughed as I listened to her groan loudly.

"Then what is the fun of a stakeout? I'll put in extra time at the gym this weekend."

"Fine then. I'll stop bitching."

"No, you won't. You'll make me eat salads and shove bottled water at me."

"Oh, Sunday dinner with the parents."

"I promise, I'll show up. I know you get shit because of me."

My secretary waved at me through the glass wall of my office, and I held up my hand. "I gotta go. I have an afternoon meeting, but text me to check in."

"Every hour if I can."

"Thanks."

"I'll see you tomorrow for dinner."

"I'll make something healthy." I chuckled as she cursed, and we said goodbye. She disconnected the call.

Time to get back to work. Maybe I could call my dad and have dinner. We hadn't done that in a while. My mom and I still weren't on speaking terms, and being home was uncomfortable. I'd thought my dad would be the one to disown me, not my mom. But I couldn't help what happened or that I refused to hide who I was.

I straightened my headscarf in bright yellow and settled behind my desk to go over my notes and tried to put Butcher out of my mind.

MY DAD WAS A POWERFULLY BUILT, DARK-SKINNED MAN, HIS head smoothly shaved because his hairline was quickly receding, and his goatee had gone completely gray over the last few years. Yet he still didn't look like a man in his fifties. We'd met up at our favorite diner from when I was a kid, and he'd taken me to work with him. My best childhood memories were under the hood at my dad's garage as he worked. We'd talked for hours about anything—cars, sports, school—no subject had ever been off-limits except for the really important ones.

"So?"

"So?" I grinned as he gave me that stern look he had when he knew I was hiding something. "Butcher is off working a stakeout, and well, I hate being home alone."

"How's Butcher?"

I was surprised at how well she and my dad got along. When we'd decided to get together and talk after I came out, he'd come to Butcher's apartment. She'd stayed to make sure I was okay. He'd known Fern, but in my former life, she'd come to hang out, but there were no overnights at my house. My parents had been tolerant but not enough to have my supposed girlfriend spend the night. Butcher hadn't been a visitor, but they'd known about her. He hadn't met her until after I started living with her.

Dad had even thanked her for taking care of me and giving me a place to live. At first, they hadn't been friendly. They'd had a small truce in place. Until she was sure my dad would act right, she'd made me promise to have him visit our place.

"Good. I wish she'd find a new job."

"She's good at what she does. She's always going to come home."

His confidence didn't make me feel any better. "That's what she said this morning."

"Something bothering you?"

"Not really. There was a woman there this morning."

"Toni."

God, I knew that tone, and I didn't want the speech. "Dad, don't start."

"We both know this bullshit 'just friends' thing you got going on with her isn't going to work forever."

I sighed as I placed my elbows on the table and laced my fingers to rest my chin on my upraised hands. "She's my best friend. I can't lose that."

"It ain't about losing it or her. She'd been your constant. You always called her before me when you were in trouble or needed any help. Who's the first one you called when your old roommate's boyfriend started making you feel unsafe?"

"Her."

"Who's the one you told about being trans first?"

"Her and Fern."

"Who's the first person to give you a safe place to be you?"

"Her and I get all that, but her job, the women, the addiction…"

"You're making excuses, and you're better than that. She ain't had a drink in two years last March."

"How did you know that?"

"We talk." He shifted on the bench seat across from me and looked suddenly uncomfortable.

"When?"

"Doesn't matter."

"It does matter."

He sighed and rubbed his goatee as he seemed to put off answering me. "She just calls if she's going to be out of town or something went down on a job. We got a deal. I'm the one to give you the news."

As soon as he said that, I realized Dad and Butcher's boss were the ones there on the nights to tell me she got shot, about the stabbing and the SUV incident and other times. How had I not noticed? I could only blame it on the worry. "Why didn't you tell me?"

"Tell you what? She knows you'll need someone if bad shit happens, and she just arranged for it to be me. Even Charlie knows to call me first."

Charlie was her boss. How much else did she do to make sure I was protected?

"You're just making all the friends."

"Charlie and the guys are good to have a beer with or watch a game."

"Something wrong?"

"Me and your mom aren't doing all that great."

"Why? Because of me?"

"Hey, don't think it. Living your truth. I did all the research, Toni. I saw the numbers, and I'd rather have you happy than fucking dead or miserable because you can't be you. I don't care who you bring home. You're my daughter. You know me and your mom never saw eye to eye on the religion thing. Since you told us, well, she spends more time at the church and with her groups. We married young, barely out of high school, and people grow apart. Butcher and Charlie even offered me a couch whenever I needed it."

"They knew?"

"You sound offended."

"Well, knowing y'all are on the verge of divorce and knowing other people knew first. And one of them being Butcher, and she never told me."

"You know she wants to protect you. You'd just take the divorce on your shoulders, and it ain't supposed to be there. We should've never gotten married, but I got an intelligent, beautiful, successful..."

"Okay, okay, knock off the flattery."

"Don't give Butcher shit for it either. She's just trying to take care of you."

"I know, dad, but I wish she'd take care of herself just as much."

"Let's have food and catch up. We don't do this enough."

"No, we don't."

As much as I wanted to interrogate him, the server came back to ask if we were ready to order. Dad got his usual which was the meatloaf special, and I made it two. We talked and ate dinner, had two desserts. I needed to make more time for him. I knew mom probably gave him hell if he said he was coming to see me. Apparently, they had enough strain in their marriage without me adding more. I knew everything couldn't be perfect. Not everyone was going to embrace me with open arms, but I'd hoped to at least keep both my parents. I just needed to remind myself at least I still had my dad.

3

BUTCHER

I EASILY FLIPPED MY SOBER COIN BETWEEN THE FINGERS OF my left hand and stared off into space as cigar smoke, and the scents of whiskey and beer surrounded me. My babygirl was out on a date, and I was in no hurry to go home. The more I told myself it was for the best, the less I believed that, and I was done being selfless. Yet I knew I'd pretend to be happy and listen to her talk about her date. Ask her would she go out with them again and hide that I was imagining taking them out to a shallow grave in the woods.

"Butcher, where's your old lady tonight?" Tim, one of the newest guys, asked, and I glared at him. He was too stupid or drunk to notice.

"I don't have an old lady. My babygirl is on a date."

"Just drink, Tim. Don't fuck with Butcher." Charlie groaned, knowing my temper was short when Toni went out.

"Do y'all call her that because she's a—"

Charlie smacked the back of his head, and the guys laughed. I smirked as I nodded at Charlie. He didn't take much shit. Most everyone who worked for him knew his husband had started the business before they met. Vic had been a bit older than Charlie. He'd come into work early one day and had a massive heart attack. It was already too late by the time they got him help.

I'd run into Vic a few times when I was in uniform. We hadn't been friends, but I'd met Charlie and instantly liked the guy. I had to admit I never saw Vic and him together. Vic had not liked me hanging out with his husband.

"Hey, Darren." I glanced back over my shoulder as Charlie greeted Toni's dad.

I scooted my chair over to give him room between Charlie and me. We shook hands as he squeezed in.

"Don't mind if I crash the party?"

"No, what are you doing out?" I asked.

"Sue is off with her church group, and I didn't want to sit around the house. I called you, Butcher, but Charlie answered my text telling me where y'all were."

"Shit, I forgot my phone was on silent." I fished my phone out of my front pocket and checked my notifications. Fern and my parents messaged, but no text for a rescue from Toni.

"She answered my call. She said she was having a good time."

"Thanks, Darren. I love to know my babygirl is having a good time."

"If you'd knock off the only friends shit…"

"I know, I know," I said as I rolled my coin through my fingers faster and tried to remember why I'd quit drinking. It wasn't for me, it hurt Toni to see me that way, and I always wanted her happy. They said you needed to get sober for yourself, but if it were just me, I'd have given into the bottle, the coke, and been dead already. I remembered every detail of her expression when I left for work still fucked up from the night before, that is, if I'd even come home at all.

Hence one of the last incidents where I'd nearly lost a fight with a couple tons of vehicle. Charlie had seen my spiral, but he figured if he kept me close, he could keep me safe, and he realized my death wish wasn't exactly natural adrenaline highs.

"Well, she's a dyke seems like — "

I lifted my left hand to unsnap the right side of my shoulder holster, and the table went quiet. My *Sig Sauer* 9 millimeters were always a comforting weight against my ribs.

"Snap it back, Butcher," Charlie snapped at me and then ordered Tim to leave the table. "I can't afford to lose any more people. Last guy is still getting his dental work fixed on my dime to keep you out of jail."

"Should've kept his mouth closed about my babygirl." I smirked at a mental picture of the fucker holding his teeth in his bloody hand — well, the ones he hadn't swallowed by the time they pulled me off him.

Toni rarely came by the office to see me. She'd been excited about her promotion and didn't like calling if I was in the middle of a job — didn't want to be a distraction for me. I'd lifted her onto the edge of my desk and slipped between her thick thighs to give her a hug. She'd heard what the bastard said and stiffened, but I'd waited until she left to take him down. Took three men to save him.

Most of the guys knew she was my best friend, that we lived together, and some of them assumed we were dating. They had the sense to keep their mouths shut, though. I hadn't officially been in the closet since I was thirteen and told my parents I was going to marry the hot ginger-haired art teacher. Poor Mrs. Hildebrand had to deal with three years of flirting until I switched directions, and I had the head cheerleader screaming in my backseat when I was sixteen. The varsity quarterback hadn't been happy when I ruined her for him. I'd had a blast at my ten-year high school reunion. Man, that boy was still fucking pissed.

"That smirk is never good news," Harry groaned from the other side of the table.

"I was just remembering my formative teen years."

"Oh, Fern has told me some stories, and I don't want details." Charlie downed the rest of his beer and ordered another round, adding Darren to the tab.

"I'll just drink one. Can't drink like you young people anymore."

I laughed. Darren was barely into his fifties. He acted like he was twice that, but I got it. His marriage to his wife had started failing decades ago. He held on because that's what his family expected.

"I gotta head out. My parents are demanding my attendance at dinner tomorrow, and I have shit to do in the morning. Also, Toni is going to demand to take something even though mom said she doesn't have to, which means I have to check the grocery list or babygirl will kick my ass."

I said bye to everyone and made my way to my vehicle parked around the corner. Charlie would keep an eye on Darren and make sure he got home or had a sofa to crash on. I adjusted my leather jacket, and a few minutes later, I was headed home to my empty house. The reason I cut my night short was bullshit. I wanted to be home when Toni got there.

If things didn't go well on her date, she'd need me. As much as I wanted her date to suck, I also needed her happy, and I'd do anything to make sure that happened. The drive home didn't take too long, and I pulled up to the two-car garage, opened my side, and pulled in. Toni's spot was empty. It was only nine, and she hadn't met the guy until seven-thirty. They probably hadn't finished dinner yet.

I unlocked the door that led into the kitchen and found the mail on the counter but ignored it. Instead, I headed for my room for a quick shower, and then I'd get into bed. Hopefully, I'd fall asleep. It had been days since I'd had a decent night's rest. I stripped on the way to my bathroom and tossed my clothes in the direction of the hamper, grabbed a pair of boxer briefs from the pile of laundry on my dresser.

Half an hour later, I stretched out with my arms crossed under my head and stared at the ceiling. I refused to check the clock or my phone to see if she'd left me any messages. Of course, there wouldn't be any. Darren said she was having a good time. I should be happy she was out with a nice guy. I swore I wanted her to have fun and find someone, but that didn't help the selfish part of me.

I'd never shied away from taking what I wanted—going after a woman who attracted me. But Toni wasn't just some woman I picked up in a bar. A woman with a name I wouldn't remember the next morning. Fuck, I felt like a broken record.

Her happiness was all that mattered. She deserved her happily ever after, and I knew I couldn't give that to her. It was what it was, and I'd do well to remember that.

4

TONI

I WALKED INTO THE HOUSE AT A LITTLE PAST MIDNIGHT. THE date had been going well, and then it all went to shit. I made my way to the hall that led to the bedrooms and saw Butcher's door open. As I passed it, instead of heading to my own room, I dropped my shoes to the floor and strode to the bed. I lifted my knees onto it and crawled up the mattress to tucked myself against her side—my back to her ribs and my head on her bicep. And like always, she cuddled me close even in her sleep.

"Hey, babygirl." Her voice was husky from sleep, and she rolled to her side, spooned me into her stocky frame. She didn't wear anything but boxer briefs, and her soft breasts flattened to my back. She absently stroked my belly with her right hand and kissed the back of my neck. "Have fun?" she asked as she brushed her lips to my shoulder, exposed by the thin straps of my dress.

She'd killed my modesty over her love of nudity not long after I'd moved in with her the first time. She said there was no shame in our bodies or the way they were shaped. I think her openness was one of the reasons I'd never contemplated gender affirmation surgery yet. The hormones and t-blockers had changed my body's shape. My breasts were a solid A cup or B depending on the bra, my hips were wider, and my slender body grew softer over the years.

But after my date, I wondered if it would be better if I *passed* more. I'd never be small or petite, and I hated how the people I went out with made me feel. The last time I'd had sex was two months or so after I'd started hormones. I had needs, and no one wanted to fulfill them.

"I went in for the first date cheek kiss, and he pulled away." My pride stung admitting that.

"I'm sorry, babygirl. Do I need to hunt him down?"

I chuckled as she snuggled in more behind me. "You would, wouldn't you?"

"For you, of course." Her hand fisted in the silk over my soft belly.

"You always take such good care of me, Butcher."

"That's what I'm here for. You sleeping with me tonight?"

"If you don't mind." It wasn't normal to sleep naked with your best friend. I knew it wasn't, but that didn't mean I fought the selfish need to pretend she was all mine.

"You know I don't. Take off the dress and get comfortable. I have an early day tomorrow. Grocery shopping and then dinner with the parents. They're not going to let me get away with missing three weeks in a row."

And like always, she let me go long enough for me to sit up and take my dress off, leaving me in nothing but my panties. We both sighed as I settled back in. She was always warm and solid, so safe. If only she wanted me like I needed her to, but I couldn't lose her. The fear I carried every day she left for work was bad enough.

I stiffened as she sharply nipped at my shoulder. "Quit thinking so much. Just get some sleep."

I made myself close my eyes as she drew the covers over us. As much as these nights tortured me, I couldn't deny I'd lived for them. She laced her fingers with mine and pulled me flush even though there was no way we could get closer. Fuck, I needed to stop seeking her out for comfort. All it had done was make my lonely bed down the hall feel emptier.

Maybe I should move and find a place of my own, but at the thought, pain tore through me at the possibility of not seeing her every day. Not getting my cuddles and kisses would be hell. She made everything right for me. It was an all-encompassing peace that settled over me when we were together. When she walked into our home, it was as if all the pieces fell into place.

She'd arrive home for dinner, never hesitated to come into the kitchen first to wrap her arms around my waist. Her lips would brush the sensitive spot just on the side of my neck. It was like she zeroed in on that single area. She wasn't the affectionate type. She wasn't free with hugs, not even with family, but with me, she touched constantly. I always had a place of honor on her lap, no matter who was around. Out with friends or people she worked with, she catered to my every need. Calmed me when I thought people were paying us too much attention.

I'd imagined so many times since she'd made my coming out special what it would be like to be loved by her. The nights she brought someone home, I had to listen to them getting what I couldn't have—their screams for more and her growly demands. I wanted the domination that came off her in waves.

Fucking wasn't unfamiliar to me. I'd done my share in my twenties, but I'd always been the top, the dominant one, and it wasn't satisfying. If she was anything, she was a top. My face flamed at how many times I'd heard a woman scream for her to fuck them harder, and I wanted, no, needed that, but what happened when we broke that barrier? I'd lose my everything if it fell apart. I yearned for babygirl to mean something more than an endearment that she always used for me. No one else got that from her.

Like this, in her bed with her curled around me, this was all mine.

I WOKE WITH A GASP AND STILLED AS I FELT HER SLIGHTLY calloused hand inside the silk of my panties. My length was only semi-hard, but she was massaging my cock and small sac as she rubbed her hips against my ass. The edge of my teeth sunk into my lower lip as her left hand palmed my right breast. She squeezed the small nipple between her fingers, and I begged myself to stay still—quiet.

There was no fight or attempt to stop her as she shoved her knee between mine to open me. The sting of her lips on my shoulder caused my body to arch. I knew she was marking me.

"Shit, babygirl, I'm sorry." Her apology was husky, but she didn't jerk her hands away as if she found touching me disturbing or try to roll away. "Sexy woman in my bed, you can't blame me."

I didn't realize I was holding my breath until she was stroking her hand up my belly.

"Did you sleep good?"

I only nodded as she pulled back and she turned me to face her. As if it was something we did every day, she lifted my thigh over her hip. Her soft lips brushed the corner of my mouth, and I almost leaned in to chase her as she retreated. She looked down my body, and I wondered what she saw, the slight paunch of my belly. My silk-covered cock. My thick, dimpled thighs.

All the women she brought home were petite with big breasts and looked like perfect china dolls. I was just shy of six feet, and while my body was slender, it was still soft. I studied her soft angular features, but she had beautiful, long lashes and full, pouted lips. She kept her dark hair long but always in a ponytail. Her body was broad, and her breasts were soft and heavy, but she always wore a binder.

"Want to talk about your date?"

"No, he was super nice, but there was no spark. It was more like having dinner with a new friend. Maybe I was too sensitive about him pulling away."

"Maybe he had a shitty boyfriend and isn't ready for even casual intimacy."

My skin prickled with goosebumps as she stroked the backs of her fingers along my ribs and to my hip. She could touch me all day, every day, and it would never be enough.

"I know, but I keep striking out on dates."

"None of them are good enough for you anyway."

"You've told me that a hundred times. There's a question I always wanted to ask, but—"

"You know you can ask me anything."

"It's always been something you've done, but why the binding?"

"That's simple, flopping around running after people and tackling them, well, I don't want to give myself a black eye."

I snorted loudly as she waggled her brows.

"There're no issues with my gender identity. I never felt trans. Sometimes I feel fluid but more Masc than Femme. My binders also have their practical purpose, they're not a distraction, and my vests fit better."

I stroked the scars on her shoulder and chest. "I'm all for the practical."

She caught my hand in hers and lifted it to her mouth to brush her lips across my knuckles. "I haven't drunk a drop in two years, and I'm more careful. Your worrying kills me, baby-girl. I'd find a safer job, but none of them fit."

"Butcher, I know that, but worrying is natural. I just want you to be okay."

I wanted to demand her tell me what started her drinking.

Why she'd abruptly left the force. I just hoped one day she'd tell me — trust me with her demons.

"What are we making for dinner at mom and dad's?"

The subject change wasn't subtle, and I let it go. We laid in bed talking and catching up about our weeks as Butcher kept caressing me with her fingertips until we couldn't hold off getting up. We still had grocery shopping, and I had to cook because that wasn't her talent. She'd eat takeout three meals a day, seven days a week. I took pride in caring for her and our home. I allowed her to come home to a clean and serene environment where she could leave her job at the door.

I needed to be her safe place whether I could call her mine or not.

5

BUTCHER

I WAITED OUTSIDE THE GUEST BATHROOM TONI HAD disappeared into, and once she opened the door, I rushed forward and grabbed her around the waist. She yelped as I lifted her onto the counter and left her only long enough to lock the door.

"Why the hell did you make me come here?" I demanded playfully as I stepped between her denim-covered legs. She looked sexy in the skintight capri pants and flowing blouse off her beautiful brown shoulders. Her dark skin glowed under the lights.

She gave me a completely fake sympathetic expression and draped her arms over my shoulders. My hands settled on her thighs and savored her warmth through the fabric. I hadn't stopped thinking about her cupped in my hand that morning or the way she'd arched as I'd sucked up a faint mark just above her shoulder blade. I could see the edge of it in the mirror behind her. When I'd turned her toward me, I'd almost let my steely control slip and took our relationship into dangerous territory.

"You'd break mom's heart if you'd skipped again."

"I know, I know, but, fuck—" I leaned forward to rest my forehead to hers and sighed heavily.

"Butcher, they just want to know you're okay."

"I'm fine. I love my job. I get to come home to a beautiful woman in my house." I lifted my head at her soft chuckle and took in her happy expression. For sixteen years, my only goal in life was to make her always look like that. Whatever it took, I went above and beyond because she was worth someone making her feel safe and special. "I haven't relapsed. I go to my meetings twice a week when it's bad, but at least once."

"And we know you're quite popular with the ladies."

I swore I heard an edge in her voice, but her face didn't give it away, so I mentally shook it off.

"I love sex, nothing wrong with that." She rolled her eyes, and I eased my hands under her shirt. She realized my intentions too late as I attacked her ribs.

She squealed and tried to get away, but there was nowhere for her to go. Her upper body bowed forward, and the move caused my hand to cup her small, perfect tit.

"Sorry." I apologized even as I teased the small, pebbled nipple with my thumb. Her lashes lowered as her lids became heavy, and a breath shuddered past her soft, parted lips. My left hand stroked around to her lower back and tugged her closer to the edge of the counter. She hooked her legs around my thighs. My lips almost touched hers; less than an inch separated us from our first real kiss.

"What the hell are you two doing?" Fern demanded as she barged in with a nail in her hand that she'd used to pop the lock. "Oh shit."

I jerked my hand from under her shirt and righted her clothes as I glared at Fern. "Learn to fucking knock." I turned to block Toni from my sister's searching gaze.

My tense body relaxed as she wrapped her arms around my neck and rested her chin on my shoulder.

"Well, if you're going to make out, keep it down." Fern flipped me off and slammed the door behind her. "Dinner's ready."

"Does everyone have to yell?" Mom yelled, and I heard dad laugh loudly.

I shook my head and turned to press my lips to the corner of hers. "Sorry, babygirl. Ready for food? You haven't had anything since breakfast."

"We were busy all day."

"No excuse. I don't take care of you good enough."

"Shut up, Butcher. You always take care of me."

"Hop on." She wrapped her arms and legs around me tight as I lifted her off the counter. My left arm curved under her lush ass as I opened the door and carried her to the kitchen. She dropped her bare feet to the floor and took a seat on the bench on one side of the picnic table my parents used for a kitchen table.

When I reached the island, I picked up two plates, rested one on my palm and the other on my forearm to fill them with food for both of us. Last time she'd tried to make her own plate when I was around was years ago, and I'd swatted her backside with an order to sit down.

My dominant side came out full force around her. She never complained, and I loved her shy smile and the darkening of her cheeks when I catered to her. I tried to keep it under control, though. My actions were normal, were since we'd been teenagers, but one day I wondered if she'd see through the routine I'd set up for us.

I made sure to pick all the cherry tomatoes from her salad because I knew she didn't like them. When I carried our plates back to the table, I placed them at our spots. Without thought, I wrapped my arm around her neck, cupped her chin, and tipped her head back to brush my lips to her forehead.

"Want anything else, babygirl?"

"No, this is great. Thank you." She smiled up at me, and I took my seat.

When I looked up from my food, I found my family staring at me, which wasn't abnormal. They all knew how I felt about Toni. I'd earned speeches every few months about being honest with myself and her. I always waved them off because I knew I wasn't the right one for her. I took care of her in the only ways I could and hoped it would be enough for me.

My control slipped, that morning and in the bathroom, my urges became too much to ignore. Yet every time I tried to put distance between us, I failed miserably. Once we were all seated, we started eating and catching up on our weeks. The interrogations began on what had kept me away.

Work became my excuse for everything. That was easier than saying I was terrified. Scared being a sober alcoholic and addict wouldn't be enough, or they'd see through the act I perpetuated every visit. I'd spent most of my life knowing exactly who I was and what I wanted. In one night, that surety disappeared. Five years and I hadn't quite found the old Aisling Butcher yet. I didn't know if I'd survive if she were gone forever.

As was our usual Sunday tradition, after dinner, we curled up for a movie night. I sat on the loveseat with Toni leaned back on my chest between my spread legs. My arms loosely wrapped around her waist. I didn't give a shit what they'd picked to watch. Any excuse to cuddle my babygirl, I'd take it. My thumbs stroked the little rolls of her belly, and I brushed the occasional kiss to the side of her neck.

Towards the end of the movie, I noticed how she completely relaxed and fell asleep. I should get her home to bed, but I didn't have the heart to move her.

"If you two want to stay instead of driving home, take your old room," Dad whispered from the couch where mom curled against his side.

"I'll just let her sleep until the movie is over and get her home. She has to be up by six to get ready for work."

"If you change your mind, you know where the extra chargers and blankets are."

I nodded as I hugged her tightly. Evening usually meant me getting home late or not getting there at all. Our personal time was sorely lacking the last year or two, especially with my meetings and work. I could've cut down on my alcoholics/addiction support groups, but while I could turn down a drink or a line or two, well, didn't mean I always wanted to.

I'd told everyone I'd left the force because I had issues with my superiors, and for the most part, I'd been truthful, but it wasn't the entire story. Word had traveled around the department about a new taskforce and the short list of officers they'd bring on. My name was up for consideration. I'd been excited when they'd offered me the job. I'd known people had an issue with me being lesbian and butch. I wasn't going to hide myself to fit. Turned out some of the guys on the taskforce took offense to me on their team.

In one night, the career I'd chosen, and my fellow officers became more than an abstract threat. Two of them thought torturing and raping me would set me straight. Said I just needed to find the right dick. After visiting the emergency room, I'd reported it, and in the end, I'd taken care of it myself when they'd said it was my word against theirs. They'd ambushed me to get the upper hand, and I'd used the same tactic to exact my revenge. I wouldn't forget them, and I made sure they'd never look at themselves without thinking about me.

I'd lost my badge and sobriety and almost my freedom in a matter of days. Charlie heard the rumors and came to me, offered me a job, and I'd accepted. Next three years, I was fucked up and careless. It wasn't until I saw my babygirl's fear as I'd walked in the house after one of my stunts. Only three people knew for sure what happened that night, and I'd kept it that way.

Years had passed, countless women in my bed, and never once had I allowed them to touch me. I got off from fucking them, but as soon as their hands touched my skin, I'd restrain them or end our night. Being with Toni? She made it better as if I were safe, and I took care of her. I didn't shun the intimacy I shared with her. Maybe a part of me kept her at a distance because I didn't think I could give her everything she needed in a relationship because of what happened. Emotionally, I knew I could; physically, I was still terrified.

Even before the rape, I wasn't the gentle, making love sort. I was rough and dominant, but since I picked partners I could use, I was safe. They'd never ask for more than a brutal fuck and rough play. My babygirl deserved my gentleness in and out of the bedroom.

Fuck, could I even make it good for her?

6

TONI

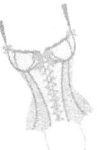

I LEFT ONE OF THE LIGHTS ON LOW IN THE LIVING ROOM AS I locked up for the night. Butcher hadn't called or texted me all evening, and normally I wouldn't worry. Yet since my date and the incident in the bathroom at her parents' house, she'd pulled away. I knew she'd had something on her mind. I toyed with the idea of a confrontation, but if there was one thing I knew, she wouldn't argue with me.

For a long time, I'd taken it as an insult she wouldn't fight. She didn't want to hurt my feelings in any way. That meant she played the logic card when sometimes all I'd wanted her to do was yell. I entered my room and sat down at the new vanity table she'd bought me for my last birthday. I studied my reflection as I laid my edges, drew the toothbrush over them until I was happy, and then I wrapped them to keep them in place and pulled on my satin bonnet.

My bedtime routine calmed me a bit with the normalcy of hair, bonnet, moisturize, and then hot tea. That didn't mean I kept my attention away from my phone, willing it to beep or ring—something. Fern had called earlier and asked were we still on for Saturday night at the club with friends of mine from work. Typically, it was a ladies' night out with dinner, drinks, and dancing. I'd wanted to ask Butcher to come with us.

"Hey, babygirl."

I looked up to find her leaned in the doorway. She looked tired but in one piece. "I was wondering if you were coming home." She still had on her vest, her weapon holstered on her thigh, and her bail enforcement badge around her neck. As much as I loathed her job on most days, there definitely was something sexy about her in her work gear.

"You know I'd call you if I weren't. We had a little run-in."

I rolled my eyes at her smirk. "Is Charlie going to garnish your wages for bail?"

"Cops should know to identify themselves."

"What am I going to do with you?"

"I could make a completely inappropriate comment." She lowered to the floor at my feet and held out her hand for the lotion I was about to use on my legs. I placed it on her open palm, and as she tapped my calf, I lifted my left foot onto her thigh.

She'd done this and given me massages hundreds of times over the years, and I braced myself. She chuckled as she squeezed my thigh, the lotion chilly on her hands, and tugged me to the edge of the small bench.

"Asshole."

"Nothing new, love, nothing new. How was your day?" As she started massaging my tense muscles until they relaxed from hours in high heels, I relaxed, knowing she was home and safe. I studied her strong, lightly tanned hands; they were calloused and scarred. I loved the contrast against my much darker skin.

I moaned as her thumbs worked the tightness in my instep and stretched my toes.

"Got a new client today. The other executive wasn't living up to the vision of what he wanted, so he requested a new person for his account."

"Did he request you personally?" I rolled my lips between my teeth at the slight growl in her voice.

"Why do you think every person who sees me wants to get close to me?"

"You're too beautiful." Her answer came without hesitation. My ego should be oversized with how often she told me how gorgeous I was and every other compliment a person could receive. The best part is she meant every word. She truly believed I was the best thing in the world.

"Maybe you're the only one who thinks so." I smiled sweetly when she glared up at me as she pinched the back of my thigh and continued working the moisturizer into my skin.

"You just underestimate your appeal, always have."

"And why do you think that?" I asked as she scooted until she sat between my feet and pressed a kiss to my knee. She crossed her arms on my thighs and rested her chin on her forearms.

"It was there that first day in my apartment. You were always smiling and bright, but the day you came out of my room, you were gorgeous because you were just...you."

"That was more about you than me."

"No, it wasn't, I pulled a few extra shifts, bounced a few bars for friends, spent a little money, but you became you. In that moment, you looked in the mirror, and all your fears and doubts disappeared. Your spine straightened, you held your head higher, and anyone who saw you could see that you'd fearlessly accepted the person you were."

"You saw all that, just from me looking in the mirror."

"You know I'm the weird one in the family, right? I'm an observer, always the outsider. It's one of the reasons I became a cop. I was good at it."

I traced the dark, harsh lines of ink that covered her forearms and up to her biceps. I pushed the ultra-soft fabric up until the shoulder straps of her vest stopped me.

"Why did you quit? I know how much you loved it. The pride you took in wearing your uniform, clipping on your badge…in helping people." I remembered how happy she was the day she'd graduated from the academy, her smile even wider than when she earned her college degree. She worked so hard going to school and while sometimes maintaining two jobs.

"You remember I was asked to join that taskforce. It was an honor to get a spot."

"You were shocked when you got the call, and we went out to celebrate that night."

"A few of the other guys took offense to the dyke getting a spot on the team. After the first operation, they made me pay for it."

The warm, loving light in her eyes dimmed as she seemed to fall into a memory, and I knew she didn't want to share; she didn't have to. I knew from her haunted look what happened. I wanted to spare her the pain of reliving it. Yet I also knew she'd held onto the pain, suffered alone simply to make everyone else comfortable.

"Aisling," I uttered her rarely-used first name. She'd always been Butcher. Even her parents and sister never used her name. I stroked my nails through her hair until my fingers caught on the band that tightly held her ponytail.

"Don't use that tone. It's not why I said anything." She turned her head slightly to brush a kiss to the side of my forearm. It was a comforting gesture. She wanted me to be okay as if she hadn't suffered an atrocity because of who she was.

"Why didn't you ever tell me?"

"I didn't want you to worry."

I'd known her answer as soon as the question passed my lips. She always wanted to make me happy and safe from the world, at least as much as she could.

"That's doesn't cut it. Why?"

She sighed heavily and looked up at me from under long,

dark lashes. "You know I was never closeted. I never had to be. Law enforcement always has that good old boys' club. You can just sense when someone doesn't like you. It resides in your gut. I did my job, and I was exceptional at it. I thought my reputation would at least get me tolerance if not respect."

"And it didn't?"

"I was respected but more often than not just tolerated on the job. My partner asked me out for drinks with the other detectives, I met some wives, and I thought everything was good. That was until I was moved to the Major Crimes Task-force. I knew some of them didn't think I deserved the spot. I was a new detective and, in their eyes, a rookie. We'd completed a major operation, and we went out to celebrate. I didn't see anything wrong with having a few beers and then coming home to you."

She closed down, compartmentalizing the victim from how she saw herself, and scooted back. She began to massage my legs again, and I almost told her to stop, but I thought she needed the connection—the distraction. I wouldn't call her out on it.

"They tried to *fix* me. Told me I just hadn't had the right dick yet." She cleared her throat and leaned forward to rest her forehead on my knee. "I did everything right. I went to the hospital. Reported it. And it was my word against theirs. Veteran officers and..." She sighed heavily, and her warm breath fanned my skin. "So, I took care of it myself. They'll never forget me; I made sure every time they look in the mirror, all they'll think about is me. I contacted the press. Anonymously. I was almost charged with assault, but they thought twice about it when I said my reports and emergency room charts would be blasted all over the news. I thought I was okay and realized I wasn't."

"You had every right to meltdown, but you could always come to me."

"I know, babygirl, I did and do, but the betrayal...all I could think about was the people I trusted to have my back were the ones I had to protect myself against. What if I had stayed on the taskforce? How long would it have taken for them to look the other way and me to end up dead? Charlie caught wind of what happened. He had some friends in the department, and he stepped in, offered me a job, but—"

"Is that why you had your death wish?" My voice broke, and she jerked her head up. She was instantly on her knees, kissing away the tears I hadn't realized were falling. Her lips were firm yet soft where they stroked along one cheek and then the other.

"Hey, I'm safe, sober, and relatively sane-ish." She cupped my jaw and softly pressed her lips to the corners of mine. When she pulled back, she smiled at me, an expression that didn't reach her eyes. She was trying to soothe me even as I saw her pain.

"Horrible time for jokes." I pushed at her chest.

"Aw, babygirl, don't be like that. It was way past time I told you. You put up with so much bullshit these past five years. You had every right to cut and run, but you never did. And have I told you how exceptionally beautiful you are in yellow?" I batted at her hands as she straightened my silk bonnet.

"You're not distracting me with your seductive ways!"

"That implies you find me seductive. Now, now, that is an interesting—" Butcher chuckled as I pinched her in the gap on the side of her vest.

"Be serious for a minute, okay?" I looped my arms around her as she leaned in for a quick kiss.

"Anything for you."

"Are you okay?"

"I'm better every day."

I squealed as she fell back and tugged me down to straddle her thighs. "You and your habit of woman-handling me."

"You know you love it." She tightly held me to her, and I wrapped my arms around her neck. "I can still see the worry in your eyes, but I don't want it there. You should always be smiling. If you're not smiling, then I haven't done my job in taking care of you."

"You do know you don't have to take care of me."

"But I'm so good at it...most of the time."

I sighed heavily and rested my forehead against hers. "You really, really are. Sleep with me tonight?"

"Your bed or mine?"

"Mine. So go take a shower."

"Gonna come wash my back?"

"I'm all lotioned and ready for bed."

"And I can reapply said lotion and to more than those long, sexy legs of yours." She slipped her slightly roughened hands under my gown and squeezed my bare ass cheeks. I shoved against her chest, and she fell back, crossing her arms under her head.

"Perv, go take a shower and stow your gear."

"I may wait a few minutes. You're looking pretty from this angle."

I rolled my eyes and relaxed as I stared down at her. "Do you ever not think about sex?"

"With you around, definitely impossible not to. Especially when I know you're not wearing panties."

"Oh my god, I'm getting up. You shower, and I'll make my tea, and I'll meet you in bed in twenty."

"Sounds like a plan." She tightened her abs and easily sat up. "Toni?"

"Yeah."

"Please don't worry about me. Everything is fine, and as long as I have you to come home to, my life is perfect." She curled her left hand around the back of my neck and pulled me down until her lips touched mine. She gave me a few soft, quick kisses, and when she retreated, I got off her lap and stood.

She rolled to her feet and headed for the door, and I watched her until she disappeared into the hall. I fell against the vanity and raised my hands to cover my cheeks. The woman was determined to drive me crazy, and she had no idea what she was doing. Every kiss and hug, all the loving expressions and words made me wish for impossible things.

7

BUTCHER

THE INCESSANT BEEPING OF MY BABYGIRL'S ALARM WOKE ME, and I groaned as I cuddled her to me as she reached for her phone. She was warm, and it was too damn early. I palmed her hip as she bent to grab the offending device and her lush ass wiggled in the cradle of my body. The only fabric separating us was the soft cotton of my boxers. Unlike our usual sleeping arrangements, I'd put on a gray tank top with my underwear.

As much as I thought it would be protection for both of us, it was useless. Sharing a bed was a mistake but one I couldn't deny myself. After my confession, I'd felt raw, and I needed to hold her. She understood because it was the same when it came to her. I wanted to tell her more than what made me leave the force, but I just couldn't bring myself to utter the words that would forever change what we had.

"Call in sick," I whispered gruffly as she relaxed and pulled the covers back up.

"I can't. I have a meeting with my new client today."

"What time?" I asked as I rubbed her soft belly and loved the way my hands and fingers sank into the curve of her stomach. Everything about her was soft and perfect. To me, my babygirl was flawless from her head to her brightly painted toenails.

"Butcher, you're not just going to *unexpectedly* show up."

I pressed a kiss to the side of her neck, nipping at her skin. "Would I do that?"

She moaned, and I almost repeated the small bite to hear it again.

"You would, I know you. Your tendency to intimidate people is legendary."

"You're probably right. And as you know, we all have our special talents." I felt lighter hearing her beautiful laughter as she turned over to face me. She draped her curvy leg over my hip, and I stroked her smooth, dark thigh. I'd never get enough of touching her. She'd always made everything right. Would she allow me such freedoms if she truly understood how I felt about her? Yet my patience and control grew as thin as threadbare cotton, the fibers barely holding together.

"We're having a ladies' night this weekend, and I want you to come with me."

"Just tell me when and where." I drew my short nails up the back of her leg to where it met her ass cheek. It took all my strength to retreat. I rubbed her in soothing circles.

"Can you take the entire night off?"

"I'll try. You know how it works."

I hated her disappointed exhale. She knew I'd never make her a promise I couldn't keep, so she never pushed me past my *I'll try*. My job wasn't nine-to-five. Not even when I was a cop had I been able to guarantee her my undivided attention.

"You need a vacation. All the others get time off."

"Babygirl, you know I can't make a promise to you I can't keep, but I'll do my best. Now about that calling in sick?"

"Client meeting," she whispered as she rolled away from me and off the bed.

I flopped onto my back and stared up at the ceiling. Maybe

I could put in for some time off, a week where I could arrange to take Toni on vacation, just the two of us. We hadn't done that in a long time, not since I'd taken her to Greece for a week as a thirtieth birthday present. Charlie owed me a favor or two.

I kept my gaze on her as she walked to her closet. I'd spent so many years trying to be good. All I wanted was the best for her, and I knew I wasn't perfect. She'd dealt with so much stress because of me. The years of addiction and my lack of care for my own safety. Yet she'd never turned away. Not once had she said that being my friend was too much.

What was I so scared of about making my true feelings known to her? I knew logically I wasn't good enough for her. She had that damn list that described a person as far removed from me as possible. In the back of my mind, there was always a small voice asking me why I couldn't convince her to give us a chance. It wasn't like we didn't know everything about each other. Hell, most people thought we were a couple. I couldn't move past my terror of losing her if I made the move.

I crawled out of bed and crossed the room to come up behind her. She tensed for a second as I hugged her waist and pressed a kiss to her cheek. "I'm gonna make you coffee and breakfast."

She turned her head to give me a quick kiss. "Go back to bed."

"I can go back to bed after you leave for a few hours. Just get pretty."

"Yes, ma'am."

I patted her ass as she gave me an adorable growl, and I left the room to get my babygirl something to eat. Takeout and all worked for me, but she deserved a good breakfast. Breakroom muffins and terrible coffee didn't count.

THE ELEVATOR DOORS OPENED, AND I STEPPED OUT ONTO the busy floor. The main receptionist looked up to greet me, and she broke out in a wide smile. Florence stood to come around the desk and give me a hug. The older woman had been a staple in the office forever; every time she tried to retire, they offered her whatever she wanted. I always joked she just threatened to leave them to see if they'd offer their souls for her to stay.

"Butcher, haven't seen you around here in a while."

"Work hours suck."

"I'm sure. My husband was a cop for a long time. Anything to do with law enforcement or whatever isn't a career but a life-style. I see you've brought Toni some pretties." She pursed her lips at me and gave me a glare of disapproval. "You in the doghouse with that beautiful woman of yours?"

"Not this week, but it never hurts to be preemptive."

"At least you learned early. Toni's already had lunch."

"I know, but I'm not going to make it home tonight until late or if I make it home at all, so here I am to say hi to my babygirl."

"You're lucky she puts up with you."

"That I am." I winked as she hurried back to her desk to answer the phone, and I walked through the maze of desks to my girl's office. New people stared at me, and others I knew waved when they glanced up from their work.

I smiled as I waved at Lucille, Toni's assistant, and she rolled her eyes at me. She didn't bother making me wait and announcing I was there. Toni's office door was open, and she was seated behind her desk. She was going through a stack of files. I leaned my shoulder against the doorframe to study her for a minute.

"Hello, Babygirl."

"Butcher, what are you doing here?" She pushed up and came around her desk.

Her conservative navy dress hugged her soft body, and I

wanted to step inside, lock the door, and have a minute alone with her.

"Wanted to bring my beautiful girl a present. It's going to be a late night, and I wanted to see you before it went nuclear." I automatically wrapped my arm around her waist and tugged her close. She didn't resist me, she allowed me to hold her when we were in public or at her work together. I'd been to way too many company things with her to have it be a surprise to anyone watching.

"You didn't have to." She took the bouquet of wildflowers, colorful just like her.

"I know I didn't. I'm going to be extremely late and didn't want to wake you when I got home."

"I just had lunch. I can take—"

I kissed her to cut her off.

"You're fine. I just wanted to stop by quickly on my way to the office. I had to go to the station with some paperwork."

She stepped away from me as she asked Lucille if she could find her a vase. "Why does Charlie ask you to go to the department?"

"He didn't ask. I volunteered to have an excuse to come see you."

"You're being awful sweet."

"When ain't I sweet to you?"

"That is true." She narrowed her eyes as I felt my lips pull into a lopsided grin, and she backed up, and I countered until I could close the door. "Butcher, what are you up to?"

"Nothing, have I told you how gorgeous you are today?"

"I think you mentioned it several times since your eyes opened."

"I must be slacking." She froze as I gripped her hip with my right hand. I stepped in close, nudging her chin with my nose. "I bought you another present, but it's being delivered to the house. Something for you to wear tomorrow."

"Will there be any fabric to said outfit?"

"Well, it is for me to enjoy, so…no."

She chuckled as she draped her arms over my shoulders. "You're trying so hard to make me a nudist."

"You walking around our home without apparel all the time? Now, I couldn't be that lucky."

"You've always been good for my ego."

"I just want to be good to you." I curved my hand around the back of her neck and drew her lips to mine.

I ignored my brain telling me to keep it light and soft, but as soon as the lush curves touched mine, logic disappeared. As I used my grip on Toni's hip to tug her closer, she gasped when our bodies were flush. Fuck, she felt good. All her warm thickness, the softness of her belly, and as always, she felt as if she were made to fit me to perfection.

What had built for so long made me helpless to resist her or my feelings anymore. I tenderly kissed her top lip then the lower curve as I backed her up until her desk stopped us. I opened my eyes to take in her heavy lids and swollen lips. She was far too gone to tell me no or to question what was happening, but I kept my advances slow, giving her time to come to her senses if she needed. No matter how much I wanted to move us to the next level, I needed her all in with me.

I lowered my hands to the backs of her thighs and coaxed her to lift up to sit so I could slip between her plump thighs. She whimpered as I pushed her skirt up to let me in deeper. Her skin was like silk under my hands and fingers.

As I gently nipped her bottom lip, her nails scored my upper back. I hated the cotton that barred me from feeling them on my bare skin, and a knock on the door ruined the moment.

"Shit." I cursed as her eyes widened, but thankfully she didn't push me away. "Can we ignore it?" I asked as I teased the crease where thigh met groin, tracing the crotch of her panties with my thumbs.

"Probably safer if we didn't." Her voice was full of regret, and she whimpered as I dipped between the fabric of her underwear to play with the smooth skin of her small sac.

"We'll talk when I get home, okay?"

"Butcher—"

"No, don't say a word, just think about it." She nodded and allowed me to move her to her feet to straighten her skirt. "I fucking hate covering you up. I'll call you later."

She gave me a quick nod, and I reluctantly stepped back.

"I'll distract Lucille." I spun on my toes to head back to the door.

"Butcher, you going to be home tonight, right?"

I glanced over my shoulder with my hand on the doorknob. "It may be extremely late, but I'll do everything within my power to be there when you get up."

"Okay."

She was confused, and I was conflicted because of her confusion, but I'd put off telling and showing her how I felt far too long. Something needed to change because I couldn't one day watch her walk away from me to go to someone else. I was over being selfless.

8

TONI

SHE DRANK SODA IN A ROCKS GLASS TO BLEND IN AS SHE SAT at the table with Fern and some of my friends from the office. I'd owe her for coming to the club with me. She went to this lesbian dive bar on the other side of the city. Dance clubs weren't my best friend's scene. Butcher only ever stayed long enough to secure a warm body, and then she normally left the bar.

I had to admit she looked sexy in her tight black t-shirt and her tattooed arms exposed. Her jeans conformed to her muscular thighs. I was losing my mind since I'd awakened with her rubbing my cock and then the incident in her parents' bathroom. The way her rough thumb stroked my nipple. I'd almost given in, and the only thing that saved me was Fern breaking in. Even though she'd pulled away, we'd still been us, but would that remain unchanged?

What made me so rattled was what had happened that day before. She'd shown up with flowers. It wasn't strange to have her stop when she was nearby, but the kisses, which were once friendly and teasing, had turned into something else. Her muscular body had moved me across my office. Her actions deliberate; not an ounce of indecision had filled her gaze or the way she kissed to seduce me. I knew if I said no or even nudged her away, she would've apologized.

While she said we'd talk when she got home, unfortunately, she hadn't made it there until I'd already left to run errands. But not before I'd tried on the present she sent me; the metallic, golden dress, thong, and strappy matching stilettos were everything. The color looked perfect against my dark skin, and as I caught sight of Butcher watching me, I knew she approved.

The heat in her dark eyes as she stared at me was everything I'd dreamed of since I realized I loved her. I exited the dance floor and sweat had my dress sticking to my skin. The stilettos were killing my feet, but the way she studied the length of my legs made it worth it. I approached the table without taking my eyes from Butcher, and with a smile, she simply turned to pat her thigh. Without hesitation, I took my seat and draped my arms around her shoulders.

My hip came into contact with her bulge, and I pressed into closer contact with the packer she'd decided to wear. I wondered if it was the soft, flesh-colored one that was slightly tan and uncut. The first time I'd found her drawer of packers, dildos, and her strap-on harnesses, I hadn't been able to look at her for a week because I imagined her wearing them.

It wasn't the first time I'd felt the outline behind her zipper, but my growing weakness made me fantasize about her rubbing her perfect bulge against my ass. I shivered as she drew her fingertips down my spine and then dipped beneath the fabric of my gold dress. I whimpered as she played with my thong.

I turned my head as I heard a clearing throat to find Fern staring at me, but was quickly distracted by the sharp edge of Butcher's teeth teasing my bicep, then just the stroke of her tongue on my skin. Shit. I reached for my drink that was next to hers and downed the contents.

Butcher's breath fanned my ear. "Did you tease me on purpose, babygirl?"

I slammed my eyes closed as her left hand stroked along my inner thigh and disappearing under my skirt.

"I think my babygirl needs another drink." She barely finished speaking as she helped me off her lap.

My heart picked up pace as she wrapped her arm around my waist and led me through the crowd to the bar. She found an empty spot at the end and pushed in behind me. The edge cut into my belly, but it also worked to hide that she played with me through my dress. I covered my mouth as a squeak slipped out as she sucked at the nape of my neck.

"Hey, honey, what can I get you?" It took me a minute to process what the pretty bartender was saying.

My voice embarrassingly broke as I ordered a drink for each of us and a bottle of water. The bartender glanced to the side, and I followed her gaze to find Butcher smirking. "Put it on my tab."

"You got it, Butcher."

"Know her?"

"She works on occasion at the bar I go to, and no, she's never been in my bed."

"I didn't say anything." She spun me, and her features tightened.

"You know you don't lie to me, babygirl."

"Sorry."

She put some distance between us, and she dragged her gaze down my body. I may as well have been naked as much protection as my dress was. She curved her left hand around the back of my neck and tugged me down; my heels made me tower over her.

"I think someone is watching us," she spoke against my lips.

"You've never cared if someone saw us together before."

"I don't, but my sister is glaring."

"Shit." I darted to turn my head to see what Fern was doing, but suddenly soft lips found mine.

I fisted my hands in the sides of Butcher's t-shirt, and I opened as her tongue stroked along the seam of my lips. I whimpered into the kiss as she roughly squeezed my ass cheek. My arms came to drape over her shoulders as she slanted her mouth across mine. Her strong fingers dug into the back of my neck and the soft curve of my ass. Her bound breasts made our bodies fit together seamlessly, and I couldn't get close enough. I sucked at her tongue as she tried to pull away from me.

She chuckled as she eased the kiss, and my lids felt heavy as I studied her sexy smirk. I was shaking as her tongue stroked along her lips, and I wondered how talented that tongue was.

"You wanna go home and let Daddy play with you, baby-girl?" Her voice was low and husky, just for us.

"Your drinks." The bartender announced and broke us apart.

When I would've turned away, she tightened her grip on me. "You didn't answer my question."

I moaned as her knee pushed my legs apart, and she rested her foot on the bar along the base. The soft denim teased my inner thighs, and she moved in close enough that her packer pushed in my hip.

"You wanna ride Daddy's cock?"

I fought the answer that wanted to slip free, but I was too weak. "Yes."

I should feel weird about my best friend speaking to me like she was, but the way she touched me felt so right. And I wanted to go home to her bed, to be there like I was always supposed to be. I wanted to hear her call herself my Daddy again or, better yet, have me screaming it.

She started cursing, and I rolled my eyes as I felt the vibration of her phone. She pulled it out and checked the display.

"You have to go?"

"Yeah, sorry, I'm the only sober one, but I'll be home soon, I promise you. I'll walk you back to the table."

She reached past me to grab the drinks, told me to grab her belt loop, and led me back through the crowd. She helped me sit, set me up with my drink, and then she was removing her wallet. As she always did if we went out, she handed me her debit card and pressed it into my hand. She leaned over me and caged me in with her arms after putting her wallet back.

"Pay our tab and get you a ride home, or should I send someone for you?" Butcher didn't rush, and I tipped my head back as she brushed her mouth to mine. I felt her small smile.

"I'll be fine. You just be safe."

"For you, always."

She took my lips in a rough kiss, and the music, catcalls, and whistles faded into nothing. I felt her groan as she stroked the backs of her fingers under my chin and down the front of my throat. She didn't stop until she hit the plunging neckline of my dress.

"Be naked in my bed when I get home."

I nodded as she reluctantly straightened, I went to hand her her leather jacket, and she shook her head. "In case you're cold when you leave." I hugged it to my chest and reached for my drink as she backed up, saying bye to everyone.

When her presence disappeared, what I'd done hit me, and I took a big swallow of the fruity mixed drink. I reminded myself I needed to go easy. I wasn't much of a drinker.

"What the hell was that?" Fern demanded as she leaned in close so I could hear her.

"What was what?"

"First the damn make-out session in the bathroom, and now you're all over each other. You been sleeping with my sister all this time?" There was an edge to my oldest friend's voice as she glared at me.

"No, we didn't...it's...wait, it's none of your business what

Butcher and I do." Her tone hurt and angered me at the same time. "I'm going to pay our tab and head home. I'm suddenly tired."

"Toni."

"I'll talk to you tomorrow, maybe see you for dinner." I stood up and put on Butcher's jacket, reached into the inside pocket for my phone. On my way to the bar, I opened the app to get a ride home. I'd wanted Butcher since I was a teenager. At first, it was a crush on the beautiful woman who made me feel good in my skin. She'd never judged me.

Maybe I'd end up regretting making the jump from friends to lovers, but I wanted to take the chance. She was everything I'd needed. Having her love on me would be a dream come true.

9

BUTCHER

I ENTERED THE HOUSE WHILE REMOVING MY BAIL enforcement vest and badge just after sunrise. I'd told Charlie multiple times if he weren't my friend, I would've killed him. Toni had finally been right where I wanted her. She'd rubbed her soft bulge against my stomach as I asked her if she wanted to go home and let Daddy play with her. I'd almost had her until my phone had buzzed with a 911 text about work.

The guy skipped out on six figures worth of bail, and it being a Saturday night, he'd known I'd be the only one sober enough to track the guy down. The house was quiet, and I stowed my weapons in my safe in the home office I set up for Toni. As soon as I walked into my bedroom, I tossed my vest and badge on the floor beside the door.

My exhaustion disappeared as soon as I saw the beautiful woman naked in my bed. I bent at the waist to unzip my boots and then straightened to strip all my clothes, including binder and boxer briefs. She was lying on her side and had kicked the comforter and sheet to the foot of the bed.

Fuck, she was beautiful, all smooth brown skin. I leaned over, my fists sinking into the mattress, and then crawled up the bed. I nipped at the plump curve of her thigh and dragged my tongue to her hip, where I bit down. She rolled to her back with a sleepy moan, and her thighs were open wide. Her pretty, soft dick rested on a neatly trimmed nest of tight black curls. As much as I wanted to find out how she felt on my tongue, I needed to ask permission.

I knew she was confident in her body, but there were questions I needed answered. What she wanted her genitals called, did she mind if I gave her head? Every trans person was different with comfort levels. I wouldn't ruin the experience of loving on each other for either of us.

I eased upward until I reached her lips, and I tenderly kissed her awake. She was arching beneath me as she twined her arms around my neck.

"Morning, babygirl."

"You're in one piece," she whispered sleepily as I gave her my weight and her thighs gripped my hips.

"I loved coming home to you in my bed." I braced my right forearm beside her head as I played with her small tit with my left. I rocked my hips against her, loving her needy moans.

She tried to hold me to her, but I pushed upward and grabbed her hips. As I sat back on my heels, I pulled her lush ass onto my thighs.

"Now, what does my babygirl like?" She watched me from under her heavy lids as my left hand hovered over her groin.

"Touch me, please." I took her in my hand, finding her soft, only slightly firm, and gave her a few gentle tugs.

I smoothed my hand up her belly and played with her breasts as she writhed under my touch. "What do you want me to call it?" I was wet and aching just from being able to get my hands on her.

"Cock or dick, you can call it my clit. Thank you."

"For what?"

"Asking." Her breath hitched as I focused on the head. I

knew the nerve endings were about the same for a cis-woman's clit. I rolled my thumb over it.

"I won't ruin this for you." I leaned over her and kissed the tears from her lashes. "Have you done this since hormones?" She jerkily shook her head. I'd assumed she hadn't but didn't want to just go with my feeling. "You want me to suck your pretty clit, babygirl?"

"Yes, please."

I didn't give her a chance to change her mind as I scooted down the bed and drew just the tip into my mouth. Her thighs tightened around my head as I sucked her, rolled my tongue around her length. It felt odd, but it was my babygirl. It was Toni, and I loved everything about her body. I increased the suction as she tried to pull out, and I lifted my gaze upward in time to see her bow, her upper body leaving the mattress.

I released her, flicked her with my tongue, and went lower to suck at her smooth sac. I placed my hands behind her knees and pushed them back to her chest. I suckled her taint and then circled her tight little hole. I held her down as I ate her sexy ass, pushing the tip of my tongue against the wrinkled hole as she called my name repeatedly.

She pushed hard, and I sat up to find her staring at me. I laid down on the bed beside her, drew her thigh over my hip as I cupped her cheek. We kissed and touched; our panting grew loud.

"You like being fucked?"

"No one ever let me bottom, but I always wanted—" She stopped talking and tried to look away. "I've played with my hole with my toys."

"Babygirl, I'm a complete top, so I think we'll get along just fine. I'm gonna get strapped. There's lube in the nightstand. That is if you're ready and no matter what, you can tell me no at any time."

"I want you to love on me," she whined, and I rolled from bed.

I couldn't take my eyes off her. She was sprawled on my bed right where she belonged. Opening the top drawer of my dresser, I picked a harness and a dildo, long and slender, easier for my babygirl to take the first time. I bent at the waist and pulled on the harness, sliding it up my legs as I straightened and tightened the buckles until it was secure. I adjusted it, so the ridge base was right over my clit. My steps silent on the carpet as I made my way back to her. A bottle of lube laid beside her. I shivered as I gave my cock a few strokes, and it teased my clit.

She got to her knees and eased toward the edge of the bed. "Can I touch you?"

"I'm yours."

I tensed as she cupped my heavy breasts and lifted the curves. I stroked my hand around to the back of her head, and her short, thick hair teased the pads of my fingers and palm. "Fuck." I hissed as she licked around my left nipple, the fat nipple sensitive, and I watched as she kissed the hard tip. She opened her lips wider and sucked it inside. So fucking hot, how many times did I imagine her sucking at my tits or cock?

No one had ever been as gentle with me. Toni teased my nipples until my breasts ached, and then she moved lower over the slight curve of my belly until she was on all fours.

"May I suck your cock, Daddy?"

I wrapped my hand around the base. "Open wide, babygirl, and stick out your tongue." She obeyed so beautifully, and I slid inside, shallowly fucking her mouth but going deeper until she gagged, tears slipped from the corners of her eyes. "Relax, love. You can take it." My right hand was on the back of her head, and my right one released my dildo to reached under her chin to wrap around the front of her throat.

"You want Daddy to fuck your throat?" She gave a tiny nod, and I retreated, then thrust forward with a sharp snap of my hips, slow retreat, and another hard thrust. Repeatedly I fucked her mouth until she was crying, and her nails dug into my hips. "So sexy gagging on Daddy's cock." I pulled my hips back, watching the length appear from between her swollen lips.

She straightened until she knelt in front of me again, and I took her lips in a gentle kiss. As much as I wanted to take and possess, I saw a hint of vulnerability in her gaze. We had plenty of time for me to dominate and her to submit, but our first night, she deserved to experience all the love I had for her. It was too early to say the words in a romantic sense, but I could show her. I was much better with actions than words anyway.

I loved the fine tremor of her body as I relearned her with a lover's touch. Took my time to search out all those hidden spots that I'd refrained from exploring in the past. I savored all her sounds and her increased respirations when I hit one of her sensitive areas. The way she arched as I drew a circle at the base of her spine when I urged her soft, bare body closer with just my fingertips. Familiar yet disarmingly strange, exciting in its newness.

Our bodies strove for deeper contact, our hips restless as we danced along the edge of our restraint. I allowed myself to be naked and vulnerable as I had never been with a partner. This overwhelming need to allow her into the spaces of my mind and soul I'd shut off for far too long.

I pulled back to find a crease between her brows. I leaned in and brushed my lips to her worry lines. "What caused these? I can fix anything if you just tell me. Are you not ready?" I kissed one cheek and then the other. "We can go to bed. I'm just happy holding you."

"It's strange." She stroked her fingertips down my upper chest and around the sides of my breasts. "Being able to touch you. I don't have to pretend I don't want to." She lowered to sit back on her heels.

I tightly gripped the back of her neck as she pushed the heavy curves of my breasts together and then roughly sucked at my nipples. I looked down to find her cheeks hollowed and hissed as she sunk her teeth into my right nipple. An involuntary flinch caused her to pull away when she began to caress her hands over my belly and circled the base of my strap-on.

"Is this okay? I don't have to touch you there."

"I'm sorry." I regretted that I couldn't allow that even with her, not at that point, and no matter how much I wanted her touch everywhere.

"Butcher, you never have to be sorry, maybe one day." She placed her hands on my hips. "Until then, I can make you feel good in other ways."

"You can. Lie down, babygirl." She stretched out in my bed, her body open and fully on display for me. I moved the lube off the edge of the bed so it wouldn't fall before I needed it.

She held her arms out to me, and I didn't hesitate to crawl onto the bed, fall into the cradle of her thighs. She moaned as she took my weight, and her soft dimpled thighs squeezed my sides. I rested my right forearm beside her head on the pillow and used my left to touch every inch of her I could reach.

We kissed as our bodies moved in perfect sync, coming together as if we'd been born to do what we were. The straps of my harness dug into my hips as I rutted our bodies in a lazy rhythm.

"You don't have to treat me as if I'll break," she whispered against my lips.

"You deserve to be touched that way. To be loved on like no one has done before. Grab the lube and put some on my fingers."

As she did what I asked, I noticed the shake of her slender hands, saw the nerves she was trying to hide from me.

"Babygirl, no is a complete sentence. If it hurts. If you don't like it. You tell me no. You're selfless, but in this, I need you to be selfish; think of your pleasure first. It's my honor to make you feel good, and if you don't allow me to do that, I failed at taking care of you. Do you understand me, babygirl?"

"Y—yes." She held me a little tighter when I rose to my knees but let me go when I reassured her with a small brush of our mouths.

Her long legs draped over mine, her dark skin a gorgeous contrast to my lighter. I was muscular where she was plush curves. Her body was created to cushion mine as I eventually loved on her, but first, I needed to prepare her. As I pushed her to the edge with my lips, tongue, and teeth, I slipped my hand between her legs. She squeaked a little when my cool, lubed fingers massaged around her tight, wrinkled rim. While I distracted her, I grabbed the bottle of slick to add more when needed.

Her lush bottom rose farther off the bed when she tucked her hands under her knees and drew her legs to the sides and back.

"Easy, love, easy." She tensed as my middle finger pushed inside. "Relax and breathe for me."

She submitted so beautifully, and I couldn't take my gaze from her face, watched for any signs of discomfort. I added more lube, scissoring until I felt her tight muscles release and allowed me to gently open her for me. I found her gland, her eyes shot open wide, and before she could say anything, I lowered my head and wrapped my lips around her pretty cock. Rolled the silky softness over my tongue as I increased the speed of my thrusting fingers.

She screamed and called my name, wetness pooled between my thighs at hearing the beautiful sounds she made. Her scent and taste, and the way she twisted her body demanding more, it felt as if I'd waited a lifetime for her to shatter for me.

"Fuck, tell me I can have you," I demanded as I nipped at the lush roll of her lower belly.

I barely heard the yes before I stroked the slender length and rubbed the base against my swollen clit. I added more lube, blanketed her body but rested my weight on my extended right arm and lined up with my left. Her hand curved around my sides, and as the broad head pushed past her rim, her nails painfully dug into my skin.

I watched her as she looked down between our bodies to watch me take her. I nudged my hips, gave her an inch only to take it away, and then gave her more on the forward thrust until I seated myself fully.

"Do you like me fucking you all sweet and gentle?"

"Please, Daddy, love me."

And I was helpless to resist. I loved on Toni, suckled as her skin, left my marks on her shoulders and chest, on her tiny breasts. Yet I always came back to her lips as I loved her in smooth and tender motions. I changed angles until I heard and felt her breath catch. I focused there as sweat drenched us and the bed. I licked it from her throat as the ridged base and rhythm gave me what we needed.

"Touch yourself, get yourself off."

She shoved her hand between us. The back of it stroked my lower belly as I made love to my babygirl like I'd always wanted. She whimpered and moaned. Called my name. I forced my eyes to stay open as I took in how beautiful she was in the pleasure she gifted me with. My movements stuttered, and I begged myself for a few more minutes of strength—of patience—and then she was bowed off the bed. I buried my face against her neck as I sealed our bodies together, rubbing in small circles as I strove for my release.

I hugged her head and shoulders, called her name against her skin as I let everything go, the demons, the fear, and just made Toni, my babygirl, mine.

10

TONI

My short silk nightgown teased my oversensitive skin as I stood at the stove making us lunch. Butcher was still passed out when I'd awakened. I raised my right hand to scratch at my black headwrap, then stretched my stiff muscles, and the aching brought back that morning—the first brush of her body over mine. Not one shred of doubt remained in my mind. Although I felt a bit of fear, I'd never let her see me completely naked before and wondered if my body would please her. All of that disappeared the minute she asked how I wanted to be touched and what I wanted my genitals called. I'd felt a bit of shame at the fear, but I'd run into too many transphobic lesbians, and I'd been irrational for a few seconds.

My hole was sore but in a good way. I'd been nervous about liking to bottom or not, but she'd been so gentle my first time. I'd assumed she'd be rougher with me. The lead-up definitely had. Yet when she loved on me, it felt like making love.

I smiled as a warm, bare body wrapped around me from behind, and lips brushed my nape.

"Did I wake you?"

"No, I needed to get up anyway. You doing okay?" Her left

hand rubbed slow circles on my belly as she peppered my shoulders and upper back with kisses.

I was never going to get tired of her touching me. Over the years, I'd savored every minute of affection she gave me, but after our night together, it was different. I didn't have to pretend that I didn't want more.

"Sore, but not complaining. Coffee is fresh. I figured breakfast would be good."

"Breakfast is good any time. You need a refill, babygirl?"

"Yes, please."

I pouted to myself as she pulled away, and I glanced over my shoulder to watch her walking away wearing just boxer briefs, muscles shifting beneath her lightly tanned skin. People would probably not like the fact that she wasn't femininely built. Fine, light hair covered her legs; it had tickled my freshly waxed ones as we'd cuddled after sex. I loved everything about her. I envied her confidence.

Tearing my gaze away from her, I finished up the turkey bacon and started the toast before pouring the already mixed eggs into the pan. From the corner of my eye, I saw her filling my mug, her lips brushed my shoulder, and she added sugar and creamer, and then she was moving away.

"Are we going to mom and dad's tonight?" I looked at her in time to catch her spinning to lean back against the counter, and she was watching me over the rim of her mug.

"Can we skip? Just us?"

"I'll call mom."

"Okay, Fern and I didn't leave on good terms last night."

"Why?" The serene tone of her voice morphed into something sharper.

I knew that voice. Butcher used it whenever she thought someone had hurt my feelings and when she threatened anyone who offended me. My friend had always been obsessively protective of me. Her protectiveness was going to get even worse.

"She asked if we'd been fucking this whole time."

"Not that it's her business."

"That's what I told her, and I got a car home. I don't think she meant anything by it, but her tone irked me. Like we were doing something wrong."

"Do you feel what we did was wrong?"

I quickly scrambled the eggs and made two plates.

"Babygirl, you're not answering me." I hated when she used that tone with me, mad I could deal with, but hurt mixed with disappointment broke me.

"No, I don't regret what happened. Though, why did you wait until now?" Part of me thought I'd feel weirder about the shift in our relationship, but when she'd started touching me, it had felt so right.

"If I thought you'd have been receptive to my attention, I would've made my intentions known when you were nineteen."

I spun to stare at her and found her watching me with that sexy smirk I loved so much. The one that was just mine.

"You're joking?"

"I wouldn't joke about that. The more confident you became in your skin, the more I wanted you. The way you were in our apartment, confident in your dresses and makeup."

"But I wasn't—" I didn't know how to finish the sentence because even insecurities I thought I'd worked through were still there. In parts of me, I was still that scared, self-conscious, closeted teenager. I'd come a long way, but the fear was still sometimes as profound decades later.

"I don't care if you passed or not. I always thought you were beautiful. Lesbian or not, I'm not hung up on what a woman's genitals are. You'd been so happy. Fuck, I always want to make you that way. You stood a little taller...confident. But I also know about your list. I'm the exact opposite of everything on it."

"You are, and that's why I made it."

She held out her hand to me, and I turned off to stove and then crossed the small distance between us. When I reached her, she loosely circled my waist, and I relaxed my weight against her.

"So, you want to give this a try? I can take you out and show off my beautiful babygirl. Love on you in our bed every night. If you don't think you want to work on making this permanent, I'll respect your decision or if you just need time. We can stick to our own beds until you're ready for us to share one every night."

"I need time, but not in the way you think. Isn't that normally what dating is for?"

"It is. Does that mean I have to be a gentleman?"

She chuckled as I rolled my eyes at her. "When have you ever been a gentleman?"

"I think I've been good for a long time. Give me a kiss, babygirl."

I leaned in, and as soon as my lips touched hers, I felt the back of my nightgown easing up to expose my ass. Butcher's slightly rough hands stroked up my back as she took over the kiss. Her dominance made me melt completely against her, arching and whimpering as she curved her fingers over my shoulders. I tipped my head back as she drew her lips down the front of my throat, and I gasped as she nipped my nipples through my gown.

"Fuck, I can't get enough of you. The more I touch, the more I fucking want."

She spun us so quickly I became dizzy, and my eyes flew open as she easily lifted me onto the counter. The cold tile countertop made me shiver, and then every muscle in my body tensed for a different reason as she tore my gown over my head. I stared at her as she lifted my thighs over her shoulders.

"I'm gonna suck this pretty clit of yours until you beg me to fucking stop."

I shook as my hands went to her hair, my fingers tangling in the silky strands as she flicked the head of my cock, tongued the slit. I couldn't keep my eyes from rolling back as my hips jerked with every sharp lick of her tongue. I moaned loudly as she sucked at the overly sensitive tip.

My heels dug into her back, and my thighs squeezed her head as she gave me head until I was begging her to stop. My upper body bowed forward as sweat misted my skin, drops teasing my temples as I watched her. She growled as my length firmed slightly and she sucked more into her mouth.

"Butcher." My voice broke over her name, and she opened her eyes; her dark gaze came up to meet mine. She surged upward, the motion bringing my knees to my chest as her mouth slammed against mine. Her left hand wrapped around my cock, tugging as I whined as she worked me until I was sobbing.

"Babygirl, you're gonna give it to me, aren't you?"

"Y—yes, Daddy." As soon as the title was out of my mouth, she latched onto my shoulder, the sting of the pressure strong enough I knew she was marking me.

Sex had never been like this. Uncontrolled and nothing short of possession. I grunted with every firm stroke of Butcher's hand until I moaned long and high and hugged her to me as pleasure broke me, and I sobbed into her soft hair as she gentled her strokes, easing me down from my orgasm.

She dropped my shaking legs off her shoulders, and her hands cupped my cheeks as she tenderly kissed me. I felt her satisfied smile against my mouth.

"Getting you off is going to become my favorite pastime."

"I'm not going to complain, Daddy."

"Of course, you're not." She smacked my outer thigh and I yelped. "Did you work up an appetite? You're going to need your strength. I have plans for you for the rest of the day. You know what you're going to do?"

"What?"

"I'm going to get our plates. Then you're going to set that sexy ass on my lap as I feed you, and then I'm going to draw us a bath. Is that agreeable?"

"Yes." She covered me up and helped me off the counter, then gave me a quick kiss and moved around the kitchen. She easily set the table with the plates I made, coffee, and juice. I waited until she seated herself and patted her lap.

I crossed the kitchen to settle on her lap. An orgasm, being fed breakfast, I didn't think a day could get any better. I felt slightly guilty about ditching out on Sunday dinner, but we were new in this way, and I wanted her all to myself. Breakfast was a bit cold and was even colder as she took the time to feed us both, holding my coffee mug or juice glass to my lips. She wouldn't let me lift a finger.

In everything she'd ever done, this was what I was most used to. I'd always submitted because I couldn't think of anything more perfect than belonging to Aisling Butcher. Should I feel as if we'd rushed? Logic told me that other than the sexual dynamic nothing had changed in the last forty-eight hours. She was still Butcher, and I was still her babygirl and always would be.

I'd loved her too long to care what my rational brain thought. My heart and body assured me this was where I'd always belonged.

11

BUTCHER

THE ONLY THING OTHER THAN MY BABYGIRL THAT I LIVED for was the raids. The adrenaline rush, the strange combination of jittery and calm. The closest thing I'd come to reaching the highs of my addiction days without all the nasty side effects. The overfilled dumpster behind a nearby bar wafted rotten garbage down the funnel of the alley. I felt a bead of sweat running down the valley of my spine.

We'd converged on the warehouse space after getting intel that our runner was inside. If he was alone, that was something we didn't know. I squeezed my badge hanging from the chain around my neck, Toni's picture attached to the back, so she was always above my heart—a reminder of what I had to go home to. The guys gave me shit, but I didn't give a fuck; I needed her there.

Charlie was at my six. He tapped my shoulder to signal I was taking point on entry. He knew it was a comfort zone. I signaled to Harry as he swung the battering ram, and the door exploded on its hinges. I rushed forward with the stock of my weapon against my shoulder. Instinctively I felt my team behind me, Charlie sticking to my heels as we began clearing the space.

Status updates came over my ear monitor. I kept my breaths deep and even, my steps measured as I took cover as one of the other guys moved ahead while I covered, and we kept the formation. I lowered behind a crate seeing lights in an upstairs office. I motioned to Charlie, and he nodded to acknowledge.

I stuck to the shadows as I noticed a figure pacing behind the frosted windows. As I neared the steps, the sound of a single voice made me believe he was alone. I lifted my boot onto the bottom step as yells of *get down* came from the opposite direction.

Charlie yelled Bail Enforcement. I was out in the open and a sitting duck. I lowered my weapon but kept my finger poised on the trigger guard. I went for cover as they opened fire from several directions, and it was none of my people. A light flashed in my eyes just as I was about to dive behind a crate as pain radiated outward from my chest.

"Butcher, talk to me." My friend's voice sounded panicked as he tried to get the other team's attention, and then someone yelled, *Police.*

"About fucking time you identified yourself," I hissed as I laid there, taking stock of myself. There was no blood, and when I touched my vest, I felt no tears in the fabric except for the bullet lodged in the plate.

If I was pissed before, I was even more so when I saw who came into sight to stare down at me with disgust. I fought the hands that helped me to my feet as I tightened my finger on the trigger. Charlie went into damage control, and Harry gripped the back of my vest to haul me away before I did something stupid.

The longer we remained outside, my anger built as my former team smirked at me.

"You should put a muzzle on your dog there, Charlie." My former commander Chad Gardener pointed at me, and I knocked Charlie out of the way.

"Badge or not, motherfucker, I'll take your fucking head off."

"What I tell you? No wonder she washed out of my taskforce."

Harry's arm caught the forward motion of mine with his elbow in the crook of mine, but I was just as good with my right hand. None of my teammates or my former commander saw the right coming until I connected under his jaw. His head snapped back, and there was a satisfying clash when his bottom teeth met his top. He jerked his head up, spit blood at my feet, and I was attacking again. The shock had Harry releasing me, and I was free.

"Butcher, stand down," Charlie yelled as he got between me and the fucker. "Your fucking men shot her. She was owed a free one. You press charges, and I don't have an issue showing your superiors our bodycams that show you not identifying yourselves before opening fire." He placed his hand on my chest and pushed. "Butcher, back to your corner."

Harry wrapped his arms around me and pulled me away until we reached our van. "Butcher, let the boss take care of it. You want to go home to your woman, right?"

I jerked away and spun on my toes; my fist connected with the ungiving passenger side door. The pain exploding in my hand brought me back from the edge.

"Feel better?" Harry's amusement made me roll my eyes as I handed over my weapon, keeping my sidearm in my thigh holster.

"We need to get a statement from you." An officer I didn't know approached and eyed me warily. I wondered what his buddies had told him about me or if he'd just seen me try to take down one of the men who was rumored to be the biggest and baddest.

"You want a statement, those fuckers are trigger happy and forgot to identify themselves, but they were always a little prematurely cock-strong. I got more fucking balls than them." I pointed to the two bastards and the scars that marred their cheeks. "Should've learned their lesson," I stroked my cheek and smirked as I brought attention to the marks I left them with; only one of many.

Harry snorted and stowed our gear in the van as I gave them a statement and signed my name to the bottom. The cop asked where he could find me, and I told him I wasn't hard to find.

"One day, I'm not going to keep you out of trouble, but he deserved it, and those two were too scared shitless to get within punching distance of you. Tim, download our bodycam footage, and I want it sent to their department."

"I thought you weren't going to show it if he didn't press charges on me."

"Yeah, right, I've been looking to fuck him up for five goddamned years. I forgot you were just as good with your right as left. Nice uppercut, but your form was a bit sloppy. You need more time in the ring."

"Is that your way of saying that I need to take out my frustration on someone before I go home to my babygirl?"

"Like I think one punch is going to relieve that rage coursing through your veins. Work it out before you go see Toni. You know she worries."

I nodded as I just felt tired, it wasn't like I hadn't had run-ins with my former team and other officers I'd worked with, but all the years I'd been away hadn't changed that I'd wanted to do more than scar them. They may have left me with mental and emotional ones. For them, it had to be more tangible, their sins marked in their flesh for everyone—every woman to see.

Their screams and mine had blended into a macabre symphony as I exacted my revenge and relived the night no one came to my rescue. It wasn't even all for me. It was for every report tossed aside, the plea deals, the bullshit man-code. I'd been a pariah, forced from my job while the people I trusted—the team I'd worked to be a part of—stood behind their brothers.

"Butcher, how about we go to the gym? I need a workout. Got some adrenaline to work off."

I nodded at Harry and then glanced at Charlie. "What about our runner?"

"He wasn't there. Bad intel. They were here to serve a fugitive warrant on the owner. We'll work out what happened tomorrow. Go on. I'll meet you at the gym after I drop off the van and gear. I want Tim to get those videos sent off before any of us go home."

I slapped his back as I passed and followed Harry to my truck. I'd planned to head straight home from the operation, but my friends were right. I needed to come down first. Harry wouldn't pull his punches, and that's what I needed. When it was time to go home, I wanted to be okay. Toni needed me to be okay. I knew she wanted to take care of me too, but I just didn't know how to let her do it yet.

12

TONI

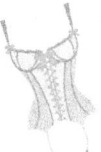

I ACCEPTED A HUG FROM CHARLIE AS I ENTERED THE GYM HE owned on the side. It was mainly mixed martial arts and boxing, and usually, the worst of the worst showed up. Which meant Butcher told me to never come there alone, but I ignored that rule when he called me. She was in the middle of the closest ring, Harry and she were sparring, and she wasn't taking any prisoners. She wore a tight sports bra and baggy shorts. The sounds of her punches and kicks meeting the other man's exposed flesh were loud, and he was grunting painfully.

She moved so gracefully, easily dodging and blocking Harry's own assault. Sweat glistened under the bright lights and made her lightly tanned skin shimmer as her muscles flexed. She had a single-minded focus in everything, her job, her fighting, and me, but no matter what, I was always first. If I needed her, she always came running, and I'd do the same for her.

"Is she okay?" I asked where we huddled next to the door and in the shadows. She hadn't spotted me yet, or maybe she had.

"We had a run-in with her old taskforce, a few shots before they identified themselves."

"Was she hit?" I knew she was, but I also know that wasn't the whole reason he called me. He knew what members of her old team had done to her. Clashing with them probably hadn't helped her internalized anger. She wouldn't lie to me about getting better but being eye to eye with people you used to trust who betrayed you in the worst way had to throw you.

"She took one to the vest, she's got a bruise, but I think they were aiming to do more damage. They were just lazy."

I shot him a look, and he gave me an apologetic look. "I like to know my girlfriend wasn't killed because the shooter was lazy."

"Rather have a pretty lie or an ugly truth?"

"You and that damn saying. Is anyone around other than Harry?"

"No, I think you'll be good. I know she doesn't like you here because of some of my clientele, but today was...I think it brought some shit back."

"Thanks for calling."

"She told me if anything ever happened to her, you were always supposed to be the first to know. Since this was minor, I didn't see a need to call Darren for an assist."

"I appreciate it."

"No need. Butcher's my friend more than she's my employee. And I know out of everything in this world, you're the only person who has ever brought her an ounce of peace. Even at her lowest, she only survived...only got sober for you."

I nodded as he squeezed my arm and disappeared out the door to leave me to approach Butcher in my own time. I'd dressed in a pair of Butcher's sweats and one of her t-shirts, my cotton turban. I looked a mess. The sneakers on my feet made my steps silent in the cavernous warehouse space. When I got closer, she must've sensed my presence because she stopped and turned. I rested my folded arms on the edge of the mat.

"Hey."

"Hey, Toni. You saved me. She's out for blood tonight." He gave me a small smile. "I'll leave you two to talk, lock up when you're done."

I waved at him and brought my attention right to her. She was standing in the middle of the ring, her padded, fingerless glove-covered hands curled on her hips. The pace of her breathing slowed. I walked along the edge of the ring, took the steps up, and slipped through the ropes.

"Are you okay?" I leaned into the corner and let her make the first move.

"I'm fine, babygirl. Charlie called you?"

"He did. Someone told him I'd always be the first to know. He thought you might need me."

"I always need you, babygirl, no matter what." She closed the distance between us and lifted her arms, wrapped her hands around the top rope. She didn't try to touch me, and even though I knew she'd welcome me, I didn't reach for her.

"Talk to me."

"All I wanted was to take his fucking head off."

"Understandable, but assaulting a police officer, asshole or not, gets you a nice little cell with three meals a day. I'd really prefer not to talk to you through plexiglass."

"He was the taskforce commander. Those other two fuckers were too chickenshit to look me in the face. But with enough balls to pull the trigger. I'm fine, and the bruise will start fading in a few days. I think I did more damage when I punched the van."

"Doesn't seem to be bothering you too much. Harry was getting his oversized ass kicked."

A heavy sigh parted her lips as she moved closer, her sweaty forehead coming to rest on mine. "I don't like you here."

"I know you don't, and Charlie does too. Since no one else was here, he figured you wouldn't be too mad at me for breaking the rules."

"I was just so fucking pissed. No matter how you think you're getting over it, it's just—"

"It's not something you get over. It's not supposed to be. You suffered the worst acts a person can do to another, betrayed by your team, a team you're supposed to have supreme trust in. It's okay to be angry; it's okay to feel whatever you want."

"But I need to be okay to take care of you."

"You take care of me perfectly, but in order to take care of your babygirl, you have to take care of yourself, too."

Her hands fell to my hips, and as she straightened, she tugged me closer, and her lips met mine. I moaned as arousal built low in my belly as her tongue stroked over my lips, nudging them apart until our tongues touched. She kissed me with possession and need, an edge of desperation as if she needed to reassure herself that I was there, that I was hers.

"You always feel so fucking right, like home." She kissed me harder as tears stung my eyes at her calling me her home.

I loved everything about her, especially when she showed me she was vulnerable because she didn't do that for anyone except me. She only allowed me to see her sweet, softer side. Since I was nineteen, there wasn't any personal space between us. I hadn't thought anything of it until recently, and I learned how long she'd thought of me in a non-platonic way.

"You ready to go home, or you want to call Harry back and kick his ass some more?"

"Home, sorry I was out so late."

She gave me a softer kiss as she stepped back to remove her gloves, held the ropes open for me, and I slipped through them. Before I could get to the first step, she'd jumped down and took my hand. Being her number one always felt addictive, but since we'd become lovers, I was intoxicated by the power being hers gave me. We'd always been each other's center, no matter where we went or how far we'd gravitated back to the other.

"It's not that late."

"Still, I told you I'd be home, and it was disrespectful not to call you."

I caught her arm before she bent to pick up her workout bag, and her gaze locked on mine. "You've done nothing but respect me from day one. You're too hard on yourself. Now, get your bag so we can go home."

"Did you drive?"

I rolled my eyes as she finished packing up because I knew why she asked. "No, I ordered a car. I knew you wouldn't want me driving home this late even following me."

She looped her arm around my waist, and we headed for the door. "You think you know me so well."

"There isn't anyone who knows you better."

"True." I tried to get away as she kissed me and tickled the side of my neck.

She made sure Harry or Charlie had everything locked up, turned the alarm on, and we crossed the parking lot to her SUV. I giggled as she opened the passenger door and motioned me inside with a deep bow. I climbed into the seat and sat there to wait for her to buckle me in.

"You're such a good girl," she whispered as she drew the belt across me, and I didn't take my gaze off her face.

The stressed woman I'd seen when I'd walked into the gym was gone. Her eyes crinkled at the corners, and there was a happy smile on her beautiful face. I savored every curve of her lips. For too long, they'd been absent, and I loved having my Butcher back.

"What's that look for, babygirl?"

"I missed your smile." I traced said smile with my fingertips. "I don't want to see it disappear again."

"It won't, I promise you. You've always made me happy. My bright spot. Coming home to you makes every day bearable."

My chest tightened as she stowed her bag at my feet and brushed her mouth to mine. She closed the door, and I watched her jog around the front of the vehicle. She was my first true crush. My best friend's older sister, who I thought saw me as an annoying kid. I'd never dreamed twenty years later that she'd be mine in every way, friend and lover, the woman I called Daddy as she loved on me. I didn't want to lose that; I'd waited so long to tell everyone the woman was mine.

13

BUTCHER

I WAITED IN THE KITCHEN FOR MY BABYGIRL TO GET READY for our first official date. I'd threatened Charlie's life if he even had the thought of calling me that night. Toni and I were still working out the details of our relationship. While we slept together and fooled around a bit, but since our first night together and the morning after we hadn't gone past kisses, touches and cuddling. We were both all in, but I also understood that she needed more time to put together the pieces we'd always kept separated.

While we'd shared affection as friends, shared a bed on nights where we needed the presence of another person, we'd added another layer, letting our strong friendship morph into a sexual attraction we'd kept under a tight rein for years. I knew what I wanted. A life shared. Rings on our fingers to show the world we were taken.

I smoothed my vest and straightened my tie. I'd carefully draped my suit jacket over one of the chairs. My binder was tight across my chest, and I adjusted my packer. I couldn't remember the last time I'd dressed up for a date. My last actual date was in college, and I'd dated one of the girls in my psychology class. It only lasted a few months at most. She'd been bitchy about Toni and Fern hanging out at my place so much.

After the first few times of her being rude to Toni and her ignoring my warning, I'd told her to leave, and we'd never spoken again. I think that was the start of my series of one-night stands and friends with benefits. I'd never invited anyone back to my place or allowed them close to my family.

I caught my reflection in the window over the sink and stared at the nervous woman looking back at me. I'd put myself in hundreds of dangerous positions. I'd been shot at. Run into a burning building once and taking my girl out on a date had me on the verge of panic.

The click of heels made me spin on my toes, and my breath caught in my lungs, a lump formed in my throat at the gorgeous woman framed into the doorway. She wore a bright orange and yellow dress in an abstract pattern that only hinted at her curves. A pair of red stilettos made her legs look even longer than normal. She'd spent a few years where she avoided heels because she didn't want to appear too tall. I'd broken her of that because my girl in stilettos drove me crazy. I skimmed my way back up to her face to find her grinning at me. She wore a red cotton turban over her short hair.

"You're looking awful sexy there, Daddy."

I motioned to my clothes with a sweep of my hands. "This old thing?" I closed the distance between us and drew her into my arms. "I swear you get more gorgeous every damn day. So out of my league."

"I think that's my line."

"You're going to end up getting a spanking for that kinda talk."

My girl was secure and successful, knew what she wanted out of life, but she still had those lingering insecurities from high school and college. Ones borne of trying to figure out who she was and never seeing herself as a piece that fits. No matter how much you built someone up, gave them a foundation of support, the person had to believe it.

"That's not much of a threat to behave."

"Brat."

"You say that like it's a bad thing."

"Nope, as long as you're *my* brat. If you're a very good girl on our date, I'll let you have a reward."

"Anything I want?"

"Anything you want within reason." Her plump bottom lip popped out in a pout, and I chuckled. "You ready to go?"

"Yes."

I took the shawl that she had draped over her arm, wrapped it around her shoulders, and asked her if she had her phone and all. After I'd made sure she was ready, I put on my jacket and slipped my phone and wallet into the inside pocket. Marigold's normally had a three-month waitlist for dinner reservations, but I'd called in some favors to get a table. It was her favorite restaurant.

"Come on, babygirl, it's past your dinnertime, and I know you have to be hungry."

I turned off the kitchen light and spread my hand across her bare lower back. I led her to the front door and outside into the cool night air.

"It's a bit chilly. You want to get a jacket?"

"No, I'm fine, I swear."

I tried to remember if my jacket was in the backseat and remembered I hadn't grabbed it the previous night. I'd make her wear it if it got colder after dinner.

IT HADN'T TAKEN LONG TO MAKE IT ACROSS THE CITY, AND she was all smiles as we were led to our table. I ordered her favorite wine and an iced tea for myself. She tried to tell me she didn't need wine, but I shushed her with a chuckle. While I didn't altogether like being sober, I sometimes missed a cold beer with the guys after work. I knew myself well enough, though, that one beer was never going to be just one.

The hostess left us with menus and said our server would be right with us.

"How did you get a reservation?"

"The owner owed me a few favors, and I called one in. I know this is your favorite place."

"Thank you."

I caught her hand in mine and brought it to my mouth to brush a kiss to her knuckles. I didn't care who was around or if they liked it. I released it and went back to studying the menu. The last time I'd been out, Charlie and I had gone to a pub to grab sandwiches during a stakeout.

"How did you get the night off?" she asked as the server arrived with our drinks, and I told her we needed a few minutes.

I waited until she left the table before I looked at Toni. "I threatened Charlie with severe bodily harm."

She chuckled and didn't look up from the menu as she spoke. "I can see you doing that."

"I've covered for everyone else. It's about time someone allowed me time with my girl."

"Mom called me earlier while you were at the gym."

I knew it was my mom who called. Her mother hadn't talked to her in over a year, and it had lasted maybe two minutes while Toni asked for Darren. She always got sad when the woman wouldn't even acknowledge her in any way. Sue liked to pretend that Toni had never existed at all.

"What does she want?"

"Wondering if we're coming to Sunday dinner, we've both missed the last two. She's not happy with either of us, and I'm not used to Mom being mad at *me*."

"You get used to it." I decided on something to eat and closed the menu, setting it aside, and Toni laid hers on top of mine.

"I don't want to get used to it. I've never met anyone who can make you feel guilty by just saying your name."

The server returned and asked us what we wanted. I motioned for my girl to order, and then I placed my own. I thanked her and asked for drink refills when she returned with our food.

"It is a talent she's perfected over the last thirty-six years. But it is true that she never does it to you and Fern. Are you ready to tell the family?"

"I don't know. How do you think they'll take it?"

I saw her shock when I laughed. "Babygirl, I've been getting an intervention at least every couple of months for sixteen years, wondering when I was getting my head out of my ass."

"They knew?"

"You do know how I treat you no matter who is around? Your dad gives me shit, too."

"My dad? Darren?"

"Yeah, he asked me about it a few years ago. I think I'd been sober for about a month. He called me to come by the garage, saying he wanted to talk. He told me if I didn't stay sober, he wanted me to let you go. I couldn't do that."

"How oblivious have I been?"

"Baby, you weren't. I never changed how I treated you. Growing up and when I went off to college, I came from an affectionate family, cuddling or kisses, that wasn't strange. But it wasn't my thing. I always kept a physical distance, but never with you. We've been best friends forever. Other than the fact I can get you naked now, nothing has really changed."

I smirked as she rolled her eyes and placed her elbows on the table, rested her chin on her upraised hands. "True, but are you ready to tell everyone?"

"I am, but the decision is up to you. I promised we'd take things at your pace. You said you needed time."

"I know, but what's time going to change? You were my first crush, I was thirteen, and you were an older woman of sixteen. You were a lesbian, and I had no chance in hell."

"I never thought you had a crush."

"Really? Fern nearly lost her mind when she caught me watching you when I'd come to hang out. I thought I'd gotten over it, you were in college, and you always had someone you were seeing. My heart broke every time you said we couldn't come over because you were hooking up with someone. I convinced myself I needed to grow up. You didn't see your sister's annoying best friend as a possible girlfriend."

"Is that why you moved in with that friend of yours instead of staying with me like I told you?"

"Which time? You're always ordering me around."

"You like when I'm bossy."

"I admit to nothing."

"I'll show you when we get home how much you love me being bossy."

I smirked at that little hitch in her breathing that I loved causing. She was about to reply when the server arrived with our food, and I moved the conversation to safer topics until I got her home. All the worries I'd possessed about us working after breaking that unspoken barrier between friends and more just disappeared. She was mine, and there was no way I was letting her go; I'd do everything within my power to keep her. No matter what she wanted, it was hers.

14

TONI

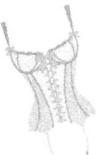

BUTCHER HAD DRAGGED HERSELF HOME AT TWO A.M., AND I'd waited up for her. She took pride in how well she took care of me, made me feel loved, but it wasn't always her job to put herself last. So, I'd stayed up. She fussed over me as I made her a little dinner that didn't come in a greasy brown paper bag and washed her back in the shower. I'd steered her toward the bed, and she passed out as soon as her head hit the pillow.

No matter how late I was up, I was always out of bed no later than seven a.m. to enjoy the quiet of the house and leisurely have coffee before I got ready for work. That's why I stood outside my room that became our bedroom. I'd thought about putting off changing our sleeping arrangements but felt silly since we normally ended up sharing a bed anyway. She'd get home late, and I'd always find her curled around my back; her warm body made it hard to leave.

I'd gotten to work late a few times since we gave in to our feelings. We were going to host our first Sunday dinner at our home. She kept reassuring me our family already knew, but I was still nervous. Yet, I put off those thoughts until I had to deal with them. Butcher had said she was all mine that day, and we could do whatever I wanted.

I wanted to be lazy with her. No errands. No phones. Just us enjoying our rare moments where neither of us needed to be anywhere. I crossed my arms over my stomach and leaned my shoulder and head on the doorjamb to watch her. She was naked beneath the sheet that was low across her hips. Laying down, she had the faintest outline of a six-pack, but I loved her softness. It was at odds with the woman I knew the outside world saw. That caring and vulnerability she shared only with me.

For too long, I'd observed as she'd built the walls higher around herself. Pushing everyone out and locked herself away to protect the ones she loved from her sharp edges. Her addictions and anger. After the clusterfuck of a raid, I'd seen the stress deepen the lines of her face. Her smile hid a sadness she didn't want to show.

She always had to be strong and stoic, a dominating force, but in our home, she let it all go. We knew and accepted each other's weaknesses and flaws. We shared a sense of equity; some days, she needed more from me than I needed from her. She needed my caring. A home free of chaos and danger. Sometimes I needed her to take care of it all, to take me in hand and tell me to relax, to let her be my light in the storm.

Our months as a couple had shown me that even without the intense sexual attraction, she was still the same Butcher. We'd existed in a platonic, romantic relationship for years and fought the inevitability of us every day. We'd still be the same two people for years to come if she hadn't made the first move. She'd thrown aside her fear and insecurities. Yet as happy as I was before the shift, I couldn't describe the joy and freedom in loving her in the open.

She would never deny me. Out in public, she showed the world we belonged together. Her fingers laced with mine. She didn't care how the world viewed us because she was proud to say I was hers. All my relationships in the past lacked the comfort of knowing my importance to my partners. I believed it was the same for her.

A smile tugged at the corners of my mouth as she reached for me in her sleep, her hands stroking over the soft sheet. I pushed away from the doorframe and made my way across the bedroom to my woman. I bent over, my hands sinking into the mattress as I crawled up her body until I straddled her hips.

"Babygirl, what are you doing up?" Her sleep rough voice sent a thrill up and down my spine as I rested my ass on her thighs. She cupped her hands over my knees and slowly caressed upward until she could palm the flares of my hips.

"I was watching you sleep."

She slowly opened her eyes and looked up at me. The love and complete adoration in the dark depths was so clear to see as she lazily smiled. "You could've done that from the warmth of our bed."

I spread my hands over her soft belly. The weight of her breasts caused them to sag to the sides. "Have I told you how beautiful you are?"

She seemed to think about it for a minute. "Maybe, but not many would consider me beautiful."

"Well, I do, but you're also exceptionally handsome."

"Okay, I'll give you that one."

I rolled my eyes at her. I eased my body forward until my lips almost touched hers. "Daddy?" She knew what I wanted when I called her that.

"Yes, babygirl?"

I kissed the corners of her lush lips, felt the give of the curves, and I teased her until she grabbed the back of my neck, forcing my mouth to hers. Her dominance and strength, they'd always lured me. I always felt safe in giving my power over to her, placing myself safely in her hands, completely confident that she'd never willingly hurt me. Parting my lips, her tongue teased the tip of mine, and she groaned as she spread her free hand at the base of my spine. A whimper slipped free as she rubbed me gently against her bare belly.

"Daddy, can I have control?" She looked up at me from under the fringe of her thick lashes. "I want to make you feel good."

"You always do, baby."

"But I want to know what you taste like. How you feel around my fingers. Can I give you head, Daddy?" I pouted my bottom lip out, and she nipped at it. "Butcher, no is a complete sentence," I repeated her words back to her from our first time. "You know every inch of my body. I want the same, but I know you don't like to be touched there, and I respect that. Consent goes both ways."

She cupped my jaw, and I braced myself for the no; she put everything into loving me, and I wanted to do the same for her. She'd had her sexual safety taken away from her, brutalized for no more than being proudly her.

"Babygirl." I held my breath. "No penetration. I didn't like it before, either."

"We can stop at any time. Now, just lay back and let your babygirl love on Daddy." I placed the softest kiss on her lips.

I showed more confidence than I felt as I got off her to kneel beside her hip. I eased the sheet down her body to expose her. It didn't matter how many times I'd seen her naked it still took my breath away. The light through the sheer curtains shimmered in the fine, pale hairs that covered her legs. I loved the sensation of them on my smooth, waxed legs, the way they tickled my inner thighs when she fucked me.

"What are you thinking, babygirl?"

I bent forward and kissed the hardness of her left nipple, nipped the peak with my teeth. She moaned and arched. She loved when I played her sensitive breasts as she pounded me into the mattress.

"What am I thinking? Well, all the years you tormented me with this body. You enjoyed nudity way too much for my peace of mind."

Her deep chuckle broke off as I urged her legs open with my left hand on the inside of her thigh. I opened my eyes to take in the pleasure tensing her features as I lightly combed my fingers through her thick pubic hair. She was so natural and confident, always ignored the disdain of societal norms. She so often left me in awe. I cautiously moved between her thighs paid close attention for any sign of discomfort or fear.

I learned every inch of her again, from her full lips to her instep. She was the ultimate contrast of masculine and feminine. Even with me in control, her presence still radiated dominance. I was still her babygirl, and she was my Butcher, my Daddy. Being hers made me whole; the remnants of me I'd thought had shattered beyond repair mended under her love. We were both broken in our own ways, but together we were perfect, our edges fitting like puzzle pieces.

Desire tightened my belly as I licked the salt of her sweat. I cataloged her whimpers and hisses and her curses as she fisted her hands in the sheet. She was giving herself up, allowing herself to be safe with me. I lifted my eyes upward to study her face as I settled on my belly between her wide-spread thighs. Her pussy lips were plump and flushed, her clit was peeking from between.

I flicked the tip. "Fuck." She grabbed my head as her upper body bowed, her breasts shaking with her pants.

I buried my face in her, inhaled the scent of her, and drew her taste into my mouth. I rolled it around my tongue. I'd been with women, but not many, and I feared I wouldn't measure up. With a mental grimace, I put the thoughts aside. My left arm wrapped under her right leg, and my hand spread on her jiggling belly. My right hand stroked her fuzzy lips; the texture and contrast of her natural pussy and the silkiness of the flesh between intrigued me. Yet, I didn't miss her slight flinch at the feel of my fingers.

"No penetration. I'll never do anything to hurt you."

"Sorry." I saw a hint of guilt in her eyes as she said it.

"Don't apologize to me." She caressed the back of my head with her short nails. I held the plump lips apart, and I licked and suckled. I took my time. This was a profound moment; she was trusting me with her body—her pleasure. Her thighs shook where they settled onto my shoulders.

I stretched my arms around her legs to reach her heavy breasts. I trapped the nipples between my middle and forefinger as I gave her head while she called my name. Her body arched into a bow that pushed her ass into the mattress, hardening her clit I trapped between my lips. I gently sucked on and off. My lower face and chin were soaked as she rode my face.

Still, I remained careful of any hints of penetration. I couldn't ruin this for her—for us. I squeaked as I was suddenly pulled upward, and her mouth slammed against mine. My cock and sac notched in her swollen pussy lips.

"Goddamn, babygirl." Our sweaty skin slipped together as she parted her thighs wider to accommodate my hips. She gripped the curves. "Rub that sexy clit on mine, babygirl."

I was nervous, I rarely got hard, but I firmed slightly. Cautiously I rolled my hips and caught her sharp gasp. We rutted. Hips rolling to meet. Sweat dripped from our bodies, and I felt the pleasure build; it was different than before hormones. It took longer to achieve.

She sucked and bit at my bottom lip. Her pussy was soaked and eased the slipping of our bodies craving release. Her hips changed angles, and fingers were playing with my hole, pressure but never entering. My heart was beating hard against hers. Her breasts were flattened between us.

"Fuck, babygirl, hit Daddy right there."

She growled in my ear as the tip of her middle finger popped inside, and it was the pressure I needed. I thrust hard against her; all care gone as we ground our hips together. My belly sucked in, and I cried out as she held my hips still as she planted her feet and rode my cock, letting it slip from the front of her slit to the back. I flinched as I felt her clench around the end of my cock as she held me there, wetness soaking the bed under us. I buried my face in her neck as I nudged my hips, riding out her pleasure and mine.

She raised her left hand to stroke along my spine as she lazily kissed me. I relaxed fully on top of her. She was still spasming where I pressed to her soaked, tight little hole. She sucked at my tongue as she stroked the backs of my legs with the soles of her feet.

"Was that okay?" I asked when my breathing returned to normal.

"You were perfect, babygirl; you always are. We'll have to do that more often."

I smiled against her lips. "Not too weird? I know you'd rather strap up."

"It was a little weird. I haven't let anyone give me head before."

"What?" I jerked my head up to look at her.

"I never liked penetration. Back in the day, when I was trying to figure out what I liked, I tried toys, and it didn't feel good. I told my partners no penetration, and they still did it, like kissing would distract me. They shoved their fingers in like I wouldn't notice. With a strap, well, they don't have the chance. With you, Toni, I want everything but—" She closed her eyes. "No, no, but with you, it all feels right. We just can't do that. No fingers or toys. I have my limits."

"And I respect those. You always want to give me pleasure. I want to do the same however you'll let me."

"Thank you, and that sexy clit of yours rubbing mine, we'll do that again soon."

I brushed my lips to her smirk as I lifted from between her thighs and fell to my side. She curled around my back, held me tightly to her chest and kissed my shoulder.

"I trust you with every piece of me, babygirl, don't doubt that." She buried her face in the curve of my shoulder.

I hugged her arms to me and turned to brush a kiss to the top of her head. Her hair was sweaty and messy, where it escaped from the bun she'd twisted it into. I knew she trusted me, just like I trusted her. I loved that I'd given her something no one else ever had. I closed my eyes as I counted her breaths with each push of her breasts to my back and relaxed into her warmth.

That's where I felt the safest, held tight in her arms as if she never wanted to let me go.

15

BUTCHER

I WAS TRYING EVERYTHING TO KEEP MY BABYGIRL FROM pulling her hair out as we prepared for the arrival of my family and her dad. Instead of the usual Sunday dinner, we'd invited everyone to our place. She was terrified about what everyone was going to say and if they'd accept our relationship. I'd lost track of all the times I told her everyone knew already. She'd been the clueless one. Which, in a sense, wasn't fair because I hadn't noticed her supposed crush.

"Is it safe?"

I laughed as I turned to find Darren peeking over the back gate into the yard. It was a nice night, so we were going to eat outside.

"Out here, yes, inside, not so much. She kicked me out of the house thirty minutes ago. Said I was distracting her."

He pulled the slide lock free and stepped inside, closing the gate behind him. We'd fenced in the backyard not long after she'd moved in because she'd always thought about getting a puppy. Neither of us had made the commitment yet. My hours would make it impossible to take care of a dog, but Toni kept looking at the rescue sites, so I didn't think it would be much longer before she gave in.

I approached him and glanced over my shoulder to make sure she was still inside. "No Sue?"

"No, I tried, but she kept changing the subject. Don't—"

"Darren, quit with the guilt. You're here and accepting. That's all that matters. I know it hurts her, but I think she's getting to the point she's understanding having her mom back isn't going to happen."

"I know, but I wanted her to come, see how happy our daughter is now. See the difference because it's night and day, ya know?"

"I understand. Tea, soda, water? For obvious reasons, we're not offering beer or alcohol."

"Tea is fine. She keeps you on a short leash, Butcher."

"I tried to talk her into it for dinner. She wouldn't hear of it. And you know whatever makes my girl happy is what she'll have."

"It's always been that way. Are we finally getting the big announcement that won't be a shock to anyone?"

"Every time you talk, I know where my babygirl got her smartass from."

He chuckled behind me as I opened the back door to yell inside that her dad was there. As she came out, I entered, figuring it was safe. I poured a glass of iced tea and grabbed me another bottle of water. As I joined them back in the yard, I saw just a hint of sadness on her face. She'd extended the invite to both her parents. I set my water aside and approached them, wrapping my arms around her waist to hold her close as I passed him the glass.

He thanked me, and I brought my free hand up to pinch Toni's chin to bring her mouth to mine. "You need help with anything, babygirl?"

"I'm fine, almost done, and you inside with me, I'll never

finish before your parents and Fern get here. Stay out here and entertain."

"Your wish is my command."

"You're being too agreeable." She narrowed her eyes at me in suspicion, and I kissed her again before she headed back inside.

I turned to find Darren staring at me. "What?"

"Damn, she's even happier."

I felt pride that he could see I made Toni happy and safe. "You know that's all I've ever wanted to do."

"Yeah, and we've discussed it enough in the past that this development makes me happy for both of you. I remember that day in your shitty apartment. Every look you sent me told me to act right, or you'd make sure I never saw her again. That you'd make sure you and your family was the only one she'd ever need."

"I don't think I was that bad."

"You were, intimidating as hell, but what you didn't notice was while you were silently threatening me, she was looking at you."

I was about to ask what he meant, and then chaos descended.

"Toni said you were being an asshole, and she kicked you out of the house," Fern yelled as she walked outside.

"I did not, Butcher. I said no such thing."

I laughed at Toni bellowing from the open kitchen window. "I know you didn't, babygirl, but you did kick me out of the house."

"That's because you're distracting. Dinner is almost ready. Come help me."

I greeted my parents and headed inside to find Toni plating pasta, two sauces and two types of meat, and a salad in a large bowl. When we'd gone to the store, she couldn't decide what she wanted to pick, so she made two so people could choose.

She was nervous about our announcement and wanted everything to be perfect.

I stepped up behind her and hugged her waist. "You need to calm down. Everything is going to be fine; I promise."

"I know, I know, once it's out, I'll be fine. Thinking something is a possibility and having it turn into reality are two separate things. And Mom…" Her voice cracked.

"Hey, that's on her, not you. You issued the invite, and she didn't accept, but your dad is here. We can't make people be okay with us. Their bigotry is on them. Who we are and who we love isn't something to feel guilty about." I turned her in my embrace until she looked me in the eyes. "You, love, are everything good in my world. Perfect from your head wraps to the tips of your painted toes. You're the only reason I have to wake up…the only reason I have to breathe. Without you, a piece of me would always be missing."

I lifted my hand to stroke her cheek and loved the way she leaned into my touch. "You're bright and beautiful, my sun and moon, and I'm so unworthy of possessing the perfection that is you. Yet no matter what this world thinks when they see us, you were meant to be mine, and I was created to be yours. You deserve all the happiness, and it's my honor to be the one to make you smile. To dry your tears. Because without you, I would've let the darkness take me long ago."

"Aisling—"

I curved my hand around the back of her neck and pulled her mouth to mine. She fisted her hand in the sides of my t-shirt and moaned as I sucked at her bottom lip. Trapped it between my teeth as I felt her tears against my cheeks, tasted the saltiness in our gentle kiss. I pulled her into me, her body and mine forming the perfect union. Curves conforming to curves. Every kiss we shared a homecoming I never knew I craved.

Reluctantly I pulled away and cupped her face, wiping away her tears with my thumbs. She slowly opened her eyes. "I never meant to make you cry, babygirl. It's the last thing I ever wanted."

"Happy tears, Aisling, I promise." She kissed me quickly and then rested her forehead against mine. "I love you; ya know that, right?"

"I love you too, babygirl, always have."

"Aww, about time you two got it right." Fern's voice drew our attention to the window and everyone's face pressed to the screen. "Now, can we eat?"

I flipped my sister off, and my smiling parents dragged her away. Darren stood there longer, tears in his eyes as he gave us a nod. I turned my head to see Toni staring at her dad. The tension of telling everyone we were a couple disappeared, and I saw her joy and relief that her dad approved. I knew that her mom cutting her off broke my girl's heart, but I just had to love her enough to fill the empty space left by Sue disowning her.

"I think they approve." I hugged her as I brushed a kiss to her cheek, and she brought her attention to me.

"Was it supposed to be that easy?"

"Babygirl, we've been together for years. We just didn't share a bed, well, not full-time. And I didn't get to love on my girl the way I wanted."

A throat clearing behind me made me turn on my toes and stand beside Toni. Darren stared at us. He looked nervous. "What's wrong?" I asked.

"Butcher, I'm—was everything you said to my daughter true?"

"Every word."

"I know I did the whole acceptance thing wrong, that it took me a while to get used to you being bisexual and transgender. There were different ways to handle it, and I know that time we didn't talk was hard on you. It broke your heart thinking that I didn't love you, but I never stopped. I'm sorry I couldn't get your mom—"

She cut her dad off, he already looked guilty, and I felt bad for him. "That's not on you, Dad. You're here; that's what matters."

"Doesn't mean I don't feel guilty. But that's not why I came in here. You did good, baby. Butcher has proved it time and again since the minute I met her that she'd do anything to keep you safe…happy. I really approve of you two. She'll take good care of you, and that's all I ever wanted in a partner you chose." Darren stepped close to give Toni and a hug, kissed her cheek. "And, Butcher, don't fuck this up."

"I promise I won't. We'll be out in a minute."

He gave Toni one more cheek kiss and left us alone. "We're going to go have a nice dinner with our family, and then when they're gone, we're going to curl up on the couch and binge-watch that show you've been dying to watch."

"But you hate historical romance stuff."

"I do, but you love it, and I get to cuddle you. That's like a bonus and well worth watching you drool over shirtless men."

"I'd rather see you shirtless."

"This can be arranged." She giggled, and I rolled my eyes at my sister's gagging outside the window. "Don't you have something better to do?"

"Eat, but no one is bringing me food."

"I think we better feed her before she wastes away."

We worked together to take everything outside and set the table, then we crowded around the table, Toni taking her place on my knee. I made her plate, no tomatoes in her salad, and her iced tea refilled. She smiled her thanks and dropped a kiss on my lips, and then I started making mine. It was like any other dinner we shared. Conversation came easily, and we earned the same indulgent looks. I knew she'd let her nerves get the best of her, but our family was the best.

Even if they hadn't known my feelings for her all along, they would've accepted us as a couple as easily. I'd loved her more than anything for a good portion of my life. Yes, I'd viewed myself as not good enough for her. She'd always appeared settled and knew what she wanted, and I'd drifted, lost myself for three years, and hurt her in the process. I was sober, I'd mostly gotten my shit together, but I wanted to be better for her.

Addiction would always be an issue; relapse an ever-present specter, but I'd work my hardest.

Her breath fanned my ear. "Butcher, you're not eating. Are you okay?"

"I'm perfect, babygirl." I slipped my arm around her and gave her a squeeze. "Don't worry. I'm right where I want to be. Eat, I know you have to be hungry."

We both started eating, and as much as I loved our family, I wanted my babygirl all to myself.

16

TONI

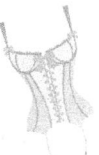

BUTCHER'S VEHICLE WAS IN THE DRIVEWAY WHEN I GOT home. She never beat me home unless she had the day off, and I knew she'd left for work that morning. I hoped she was in one piece. I parked and got out, slammed the door, and made my way to the porch. The front door opened before I got to it. She was standing inside in a tight sports bra and baggy workout shorts. Flickering firelight backlit her, and I became suspicious.

"You're home early," I said as I stepped inside and stopped beside her. I sighed as she pinched my chin and brought my mouth down to hers.

"I have a surprise for you, babygirl. I think you deserve a bit of pampering." She took my briefcase and set it on the table beside the door, threw my keys in the key bowl that she'd rolled her eyes at when she'd mistakenly put me in charge of decorating when I moved in.

I hummed my approval. For three weeks, I'd pulled long days working on my client's newest campaign, and we'd finally gotten his go-ahead to run with it. There was always stress when collaborating with a new client, especially one who had already had an unpleasant experience with one of my coworkers.

"What do you have planned, Daddy?" I whispered as she swept me farther inside. I froze at the rearranged living room that had the couch and coffee table moved out of the way. A palette of blankets and towels was on the rug in front of the fireplace, as well as a line of bottles and a few other towels along with one of my cotton headwraps. There were also electric candles dimly illuminating the room.

"My babygirl is going to get in the tub, and you're going to let me bathe you, and then I'm going to give you a very long massage. Does that sound good, babygirl?"

"It sounds perfect."

"I need your phone."

I didn't hesitate to hand it over, and she plugged it in, turned it on silent. I noticed hers was already on the table. She took my hands and drew me toward the hall, then to my bedroom. Her gaze never left mine, and once we entered the bathroom, she dropped to her knees and sat back on her heels. She removed my left shoe and set my bare foot on her thigh.

She touched me with such reverence and care as if I were truly precious. Her lips brushed my knee as she reached under my skirt, her fingertips skimming the inside and outside of my thigh. I moaned as she deftly unhooked my stocking from my garter belt and repeated the agonizingly slow actions on the other. I combed her long hair back from her face. She rarely wore it loose, and I loved the raw silk of the strands dancing in the hollows between my fingers. I studied every angle and curve, the tiny lift of her lush lips. I traced the lines beside her eyes.

"What are you thinking about?" she asked as she hooked her fingers in the sides of my thong and drew it down my legs.

"How lucky I am." I gasped as she nuzzled me through my skirt.

"Oh, baby, I am the lucky one," she whispered as she got to her feet and stood in front of me. "I thought about this all day since I sent you to work." The desire and need were clear in her voice as she began to release the buttons on my blouse.

She teased me with a kiss she denied. A soft, barely-there caress to my lips only to retreat when I moved in for more. I pouted at her sexy smirk. When she reached my waist, she tugged my shirt free, slipping the last few buttons free. She pushed it off my shoulders to fall to the floor behind me.

"Do you even know how much I missed you today?" She finally kissed me like I wanted, the tip of her tongue nudging my lips apart, and I hugged her close as our warm skin met.

I barely registered my skirt loosening and dropping to my feet. A deep groan rumbled her chest as she undid the front catch of my bra, and I was naked, my softer body pressed to her more angular one. She palmed my tiny breasts and played with my pebbled nipples. She deepened the kiss, turned rougher as she rubbed me against her bare belly.

"Aisling," I whimpered as she retreated but only long enough to tip my chin up with her nose, licked down the front of my throat. Tongued the hollow between my collarbones and lower until she suckled at one nipple then the other, plumping the small curves. Tremors worked through my body from head to toe as I buried my face in her hair, inhaled the scent of her shampoo, and the masculine fragrance of her favorite cologne, faded after hours of wear.

I loved the way she made me feel. Always tender and adoring when she touched me—looked at me. All the pieces I'd tried to compartmentalize, my slight insecurities; none of that mattered. I saw myself through her eyes. Years of indecision and gender dysphoria, the parts of me I didn't see as feminine felt soft and right when she caressed them. Comparisons made through the visions of society and media that told me I was too tall, too strongly built—too oversized, but in her hands, I fit.

Two pieces who had always aligned. I arched into her touch as she smoothed the backs of her fingers up my stomach. She turned away to fill the clawfoot tub she'd paid a fortune for because I'd wanted it, and I couldn't take my eyes off her. I was fascinated by the play of muscles shifting and contracting under her tanned and tattooed skin. I counted the scars and freckles, took in the rolls along her ribs. In the months we'd been a couple, I cataloged them all with my fingers and lips. I knew her body as well as my own.

She added my favorite bath oil, checked the temperature, and adjusted before turning her upper body, and held out her hand for me. She helped me into the tub, and I sank into water that was just right. She cupped the back of my neck to put the pillow behind my head and got me all settled in.

"Tell me all about your day, babygirl, don't leave out a detail."

Before she turned off the water, she wet a rag to gently clean off my makeup. Washing away my day and the stress, as I talked, she bathed me gently, never lingering long enough to purposely arouse but to tease. A soft moan escaped as she washed between my legs, and I opened them wider for her.

She chuckled, and I glared at her. "None of that, babygirl. I still have a lot of plans for you."

"How did you get another day off?" I asked as she finished, wrung out the rag, and draped it over the side of the tub.

"I told Charlie that my girl deserved my undivided attention. I told him I need more time to focus on you and that I'd waited a long time to tell everyone you were mine. While I can't guarantee a lot of early evenings or weekends off, there'll definitely be more."

"You know you don't have to change for me. While I'm not a fan of your schedule most of the time, I know you love your job."

She stroked my cheek with the backs of her fingers and then

traced my bottom lip with the slightly rough pad of her thumb. "But you deserve the time and respect. Also, I've covered for people so many times, about time they returned the favors."

"It meant everything to come home to you waiting for me. Planning a night for me."

"I love you, babygirl. Making you happy makes me happy." She lifted and leaned over the side of the tub. Her hand caressed my short hair as her mouth came down on mine. I felt her smile against my lips as I tried to coax her into the tub with me. "You're aiming for a spanking instead of a massage now."

"But, Daddy, I can make it up to you. You know what my favorite thing is." A shuddered breath and high-pitched squeak passed my lips as she cupped my cock. "Let me make you feel good, please."

"Not until I finish with you."

I panted as she played around my hole, and I dug my nails into her upper back as I rolled my hips, trying to get more contact. I glared as she chuckled and pulled away. She lived to torture me. She handed me my shower cap and ordered me to rinse off, and then she'd dry me. I'd take any excuse to have her hands on me. She gave amazing massages, but she'd never set up one like she had planned.

I put on my shower cap and rinsed off; I didn't linger like I normally would. I was a fan of long, hot showers. I turned off the water and pushed the curtain aside. A small smile tugged at the corners of my lips to find her waiting there with a towel. She dried me off and then wrapped it around me.

Once again, she slowly led me back to the living room. She lowered me to the soft pallet she'd made and settled between my legs, draping them over hers as she sat back on her heels. She reached for the bottles of massage oil that were sitting on a warmer. She poured some into her hand, and I arched as her slick hands stroked from my hips, around to push under my back to arch me to allow her freedom.

A tremor worked through my body as she worked along my spine, long, deep strokes of her fingers, and I sighed as even more stress faded away. She moved, and I hissed as the soft bulge of her packer nudged my sac, pushed between my ass cheeks to tease my hole. There was silence except for the quickening of our breaths as my ass moved farther up her thighs.

A whimper escaped as she caressed around to my belly. She only stopped long enough to add more oil, and she massaged my hips and pelvis, her thumbs teasing the head of my cock. She didn't linger, just drew those strong hands upward until she played with the curves of my chest. I shivered and arched painfully as she focused on my sensitive nipples.

"Keep your eyes closed and just enjoy." Her voice huskier, and she removed her touch, I assumed to slick her hands, but then she was back, bent forward until her hard nipples were grazing my belly. I cupped the sides, circled the distended peaks with my thumbs as she massaged the curves of my ass, slipping into my crease.

I lost track of time. How did you measure time with pants and moans, the easing of work tensed muscles? I submitted my body to her will. Allowed her to take care of me because it was what made her happy. Did she understand that giving myself to her dominance was what made me free?

I touched her wherever I could reach until she moved away to deeply work the muscles of my legs, all the way to my feet. She placed my ankles on her shoulders, and my ass rubbed against her bare belly. Nothing existed but us in that moment. No work. No specter of the past. No insecurities. It was simply her loving on me. It was perfect, and I never wanted it to end.

17

BUTCHER

I SMIRKED UP AT TONI WHERE SHE SAT ON MY DESK AS I slipped my hand under her skirt and teased her inner thigh. She hissed at me and tried to cross her legs, which just trapped my fingers. She'd come by with lunch. The guys were giving us shit, and Tim thankfully kept his mouth shut. The kid was learning.

"You do know the bathroom is close by, and it has a lock?" Harry asked from behind his computer screen. He peeked around the edge, and I flipped him off.

The front door opened, and we looked through the grates and the bulletproof glass that separated the reception area from our chaos of desks. I snarled as I saw my former commander on the other side. I didn't bother moving from where I had my feet propped on the desk, but I did remove my hand from under Toni's dress. She moved a little closer to me and I draped my arm over her lap.

We all stared at the man as he knocked, and none of us bothered getting up, everyone else went back to work, but I just watched his face turn redder. Surprisingly, there hadn't been repercussions from the hit I gave him, but I think that had more to do with department PR and the District Attorney's office not wanting to deal with it.

"He looks a little...flushed," Toni whispered.

I didn't have time to comment before Charlie exited his office. "No one is going to show the nice, polite policeman in?"

All of us answered nope, and he rolled his eyes as we batted our lashes like we always did. He liked to bitch he was more babysitter than boss. I never took my attention off Gardener as Charlie approached the steel-reinforced door and opened it to let the other man in.

"You have a warrant?" Charlie asked.

"Do I need one?"

Charlie bent and motioned him in with a flourish of his arm. "Welcome. How may we assist you today?"

I laughed as my friend put on his best polite receptionist voice. He slipped the bar back into place as Gardener, in his jeans, t-shirt, and leather jacket, stood at the edge of our work area. We weren't the most organized, especially since we didn't spend much time in the building. Our mobile units were our home away from home.

"Do I need to go?" Toni asked.

Even though we all looked relaxed, tension thickened in the air. I turned to Toni with a smile, reached up to pinch her adorable chin, and brought her mouth down to mine. "You keep that sexy ass right where it is. I still have twenty minutes with you."

She nodded as she laid her arm over mine to lace our fingers, and I savored her silent support. After the raid, I became stricter about my meetings. I'd gone to once a week but was back up to two, sometimes three. I still hated the constant acknowledgment of my addictions. Every meeting drained me of my mental energy, and when I got home Toni would open her arms, and I was okay again.

"Butcher, can we have a minute?" Gardener asked.

"Sure, go ahead."

"In private."

"Not happening. Remember last time or the time before that? Because I do."

He blew out a heavy breath, and I glanced around to find my team turned their chairs to glare him down. Sometimes we clashed, drew blood in and out of the ring, but I knew I didn't have to worry about having any of them at my six.

"I'm...sorry."

"Excuse me, what was that?" I held my hand behind my ear and leaned forward a little.

Gardener growled as he shoved his hands into his pockets. "Don't be an asshole, Butcher. Fuck, you're worse than you were as a cop."

"Thanks." I squeezed my fingers around Toni's as she snorted and tried to cover it with a cough.

"I don't have to like my team, most of the time, I hate them, but they were assigned to me because they were the best of the best. You were assigned to me because you were the best and still are."

"Investigating me, do I need a lawyer?"

"Shut the fuck up." He huffed; Toni sounded scarier than him. "I can't change the past, can't go back five years and do the right fucking thing. Whether I pushed or not, the bosses weren't going to let their new elite taskforce get taken down on your word."

"Apologies are meaningless. You regret what they did, but that doesn't change they still have their badges, and I don't. I was a good cop. Who I fucked or loved shouldn't have factored in."

He tipped his head back and sighed. When he lifted his head, he scrubbed his hands over his face. "Do you want your badge back?"

The suddenness of the question took me by surprise. I let

my gaze move around the room and everyone stared at me. Charlie and Harry's looks were the heaviest of them. Charlie knew my past, and Harry assumed or had heard the rumors, too, but he'd never came straight out and asked why I'd quit. Toni's nails made soothing circles on my arm.

Did I want my job back? If they'd asked me that after they'd done the right thing, I would've jumped at the chance, but that trust no longer existed. I couldn't make entry into a building and feel confident the team behind me would make sure I made it home.

"No." As soon as the word was out, Charlie and Harry visibly relaxed. Toni would go along with whatever choice I made. They all knew how proud I was of my job and the people I helped. I'd worn my uniform with pride. Clipped on my detective shield for a year, knowing I'd accomplished my goal. The past was that, and it needed to stay there.

"No?"

A bitter laugh slipped free. "What did you think I was gonna do, Gardener? Jump at the chance to work on a team where two of the members thought the right dick would fix me —" I felt the tension go up several notches. "—no, if our superiors had fired them and the DA had filed charges, then maybe I would've said yes. That's not the case. I shouldn't have to be worried if someone is gonna have my back. So, no, I don't want my badge back. Someone send you to ask?"

"I came on my own. We were never friends. I was your boss, I'm not there to make nice with the people on my taskforce, but I know a good cop when I see them. You were above reproach."

"Doesn't change what happened, man. Doesn't change that two of your men have my initials branded into their chests to remind them they fucked with the wrong person. I'll never forget them, and they damn sure won't forget me." Toni's hand tightened almost painfully on mine, and I glanced up at her to find her watching me with horror. I'd never shared the extent of my revenge or the fact I was threatened with a good chunk of time for what I'd done.

When she leaned forward, I tipped my head back, and her lips brushed mine. Gardener cleared his throat and made Toni flinch. I shot him a look making sure he knew I didn't appreciate it.

"Neither of them fessed up, but both were put on leave without pay for what happened at the raid. It doesn't mean much, I know, but I was sorry to lose you."

"No, it doesn't mean much." He didn't look surprised by my reply. Being a known asshole had its perks.

"You did get a free shot at me. That must've made you happy."

"You didn't lose any of those pretty teeth. I'll have to work on it for next time."

"Next time, you'll be in cuffs."

"You're not my type, Gardner." As soon as I said it, he cut his eyes to my girl, and I dared his ass to say something. He would lose teeth then.

"Butcher." Charlie sharply said my name, and I realized my right hand was already curled into a tight fist.

"No paying for dental work...promise," I begrudgingly assured him.

"Thank you, my bank account would appreciate it."

"Have we said our piece and made friends now, maybe want to hug it out?" Harry asked. "If Butcher doesn't want to, I can sacrifice myself. It would be so hard on me."

I nearly lost it as I saw Gardener back up to the door when Harry stood and started toward him. "He wants me. He looked at my ass the night of the raid. It's okay. I'll be gentle." Harry was almost in touching range. There was another rough clearing of a throat, and Charlie opened the door. The man couldn't get through the door fast enough. Everyone laughed as the front door slammed, and Charlie slid the bar back into place.

"You have terrible taste in men," I told my friend.

"Ain't that the fucking truth," he said with a loud snort and headed for the coffeepot.

I dropped my feet to the floor and turned until I was positioned so I could wedge my upper body between her thighs. "You're going to be late going back to work."

She slouched forward to rest her forehead on mine. "I'll be fine. You needed me here. Are you okay?"

"I'm good, babygirl." I rubbed the sides of her thighs with my thumbs and tipped my head back to give her a gentle kiss. I smiled up at her as she rested her forearms on my shoulders.

"You going to be home at a decent hour?"

"You gotta ask Charlie that one."

"You gonna have my Daddy home on time?" she asked with a huge, innocent smile, and Charlie instantly choked on his coffee.

"Brat," I whispered, and she shrugged.

"I love you. I'll see you whenever you get home. I'll keep the bed warm for you."

"Do that. And I love you too, baby." As she started to slip off my desk, I was on my feet to give her a proper goodbye and ignored the wolf whistles going on. I barely let her go. She said bye to everyone and then made a show of passing Charlie while he tried to clear coffee from his airway.

"You've corrupted a nice, decent girl," Charlie accused. "I should tell Darren."

"I think Darren already knows."

I went back to work with thoughts of getting home to my girl on time. I wished my job allowed for more time and regular hours, but if there was one thing I knew, I couldn't survive a nine-to-five office job. She told me I shouldn't stress over my hours. We'd had the same schedule for years. It worked for us, and we cherished the time we did get together. That didn't mean I couldn't demand time; an idea popped into my head, and I got to planning.

18

TONI

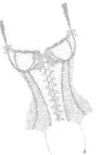

No matter what they said about women loving to shop, it didn't apply to me, but Fern and I had spent less time together lately. Butcher had sent me off for a girl's day; she told me I deserved it. I didn't miss her telling me to buy something pretty for her to take off me.

"That grin of yours is just creepy," Fern said, and my cheeks heated as I realized the thought of Butcher getting me naked had made me smile.

"Butcher told me to buy something pretty."

"You mean she told you to buy something sexy and minimal."

I could've done something mean and told her Butcher preferred me naked, and I was tempted just to make her uncomfortable. For a family who was extremely sex-positive, Fern got a bit embarrassed about sex. We'd long ago made a pact to never talk about our sex lives, and the fact I was dating her sister made it too easy to mortify her. "Probably." I chuckled as my best friend groaned. "How's everything going?"

"Except for my best friend abandoning me at lunch for afternoon quickies with my sister —"

"There are no afternoon quickies. I take her lunch when I can, sit on her desk, and try to keep her hand out from under my skirt. But seriously, I was assigned a new account. He loved a campaign so much that he's been having us work on stuff regularly. You know what Butcher's hours are? Sometimes lunch is the best time to spend a few minutes together."

"How's that going for you? Butcher being—" She paused as she sent me a cautious look.

"She's good to me." I hated that I sounded defensive. I understood the worry Butcher's family carried around, but she didn't deserve to have her every action analyzed. They didn't mean anything by it, and I tried to remind myself of that. I didn't want to fight with Fern.

"I know she's good to you, but roommates to lovers, well, that's different. Her work hours. Her job isn't safe."

"No, it's not, but as I tell her, she loves her job as much as I do mine. She's not meant for some office drone job. She'd be miserable. But she's been taking off nights and weekends lately. One night I came home to her having the living room lit up with candles. She gave me a bath and an hour-long massage."

"Butcher? Aisling Butcher takes off time and gives baths."

"She gives a lot of baths. Does my hair. Feeds me. She caters to my every need."

"Um, wow, that's…that's nice."

"Do you have a problem with Butcher and me dating? You didn't seem to when we had family dinner at our place."

"No, no, it's just weird. Not weird, dammit, I'm not doing this right." She stopped looking through dresses and turned toward me. She let out the loudest huff I'd ever heard.

"Just say what's on your mind."

"She's always had a soft spot for you. And you weren't really covert about your crush back when we were in school. And over the years, she makes your plates, she hyper focuses on you, but…but when she was drinking and whatever else she was doing, I saw how hurt you were, how it broke your heart. There's a chance of relapse."

"Which I'm well aware, she goes to two meetings a week. She doesn't promise me she'll stay sober. It's always a danger, but she's worth it. And you and mom and dad need to relax the worry. She gets that you're concerned about her, but every time she comes around, she can see you speculating. Why would she want to visit when you're just watching her for signs?"

"Shit, have we been that bad?" She frowned as she hugged the armful of items to her chest.

"You asked me over lunch like clockwork."

"So she's been avoiding us?" I nodded. "Well, that sucks. I'll talk to the parents."

"Thanks."

"I'm sorry."

"I get it. I do. I worry, too. She's in a good place, Fern. She's working on things at her own pace."

"She is. I don't think she would've gotten sober without having you. When I'd come over to her apartment when you were in college, and you were living with her, her shitty apartment turned into a home. She'd come home with a present for you. I think she bought you an entire wardrobe."

"I had more clothes than one person needed. She has good taste. She bought me that gold dress I wore at the club."

"No, she bought herself that dress. Was that the night she made the first move?"

"No, a few days before that, she came to the office to bring me flowers."

"I just can't picture my sister, asshole extraordinaire, bringing flowers and planning romantic nights." She shook her head and went back to looking for her size.

I wasn't experiencing the same luck in finding anything I liked. Outside of girls' nights out, I didn't go out all that much. Butcher had taken me on several dates, but mostly we ordered takeout and spent time curled up on the couch. We spent so much time apart that we just wanted to be with each other when we did get time. Pretty lingerie I could always buy. My woman had a weakness for me in garter belts, silk stockings, and stilettos, and nothing else. She loved me naked but enjoyed getting to unwrap me, though.

"There's that grin again."

"I was just thinking about how much Butcher likes to unwrap me."

"You're hopeless."

"My woman is sexy, what she can do with her ton—"

I lost it as Fern screamed and covered her ears. Everyone in the store looked around, panicked. I wrapped my hands around her wrists and pulled her hands from her ears.

"You're too easy."

"And my sister has completely corrupted my best friend, but that's not anything new. Now tell me everything that I've missed out on hearing about during our lunches."

I took pity on her and kept the topics safe—work and my new client. Told her I was up for a senior promotion. I found three pretty dresses but spent most of my budget on panties, bras, garter belts, and stockings. Out of all the clothes I'd ever worn, it was the tiny slips of lace and silk I'd always felt the most comfortable in. Butcher had shown me for years that my body was beautiful, and I should show it off, but in her words, not too much. Although, that was a newer inclination. She believed everyone found me irresistible.

"How much lingerie do you need?" Fern asked from beside me as the cashier told me the total.

"I think the obsession was borne of jealousy."

"Jealousy, unless it comes to Butcher, you were never a jealous person."

I hesitated to answer her question as I paid for my purchases and waited for the sales lady to bag them up. We left the store and headed toward our usual next stop—a coffee stand in the middle of the mall.

"I envied you went you got your first bra. When you started to develop curves. I compared my painfully skinny body to yours."

"Toni, why didn't you ever say something?"

"I'd told you I liked boys and girls, but the other thing I tried to ignore until it was excruciating to hide it. I wanted my body to change so much to reflect who I was. Then Butcher bought me my first bra at sixteen. You know it wasn't anything fancy, just some silk and lace. It was amazing, though. So, I have a little silk and lace fetish."

"And you're dating a woman who wears boxers and binders."

"Which she's exceptionally sexy in." I laughed as she bumped me with her shoulder. "And out of."

"I will scream again. If you were talking about any woman other than my sister, I'd probably be okay, but…I've spent the night at her place before. I got up in the middle of the night and went home."

"She does have a thing for screamers."

"Not going to have that conversation. Toni?"

I turned to glance down at her. "Yeah?"

"I'm really happy for you and Butcher, especially you. No one was clueless she had feelings for you. Yet we were surprised that she gave in."

"I was, too, at first. You're best friends and roommates with someone for so long that you think you know everything about someone. I was scared at first. I didn't want to lose her, but I can't imagine not being hers, Fern. No matter what the future holds, I won't regret it."

"I know you won't. You were already acting like a girlfriend; you just didn't get the benefits."

"Oh, I got plenty of benefits before. They're even better now, though."

"You just can't help yourself."

"I really can't, some people get all adorable when they blush, but that shade of red on you, not so much."

She gave me an offended huff and picked up her pace. I caught up with her; she was a head shorter than me. Butcher got all the height and left little over for Fern. We ordered coffee and window shopped as we drank it. By the time we finished with our shopping trip, I'd used up two months of clothes budget. I didn't feel guilty about it. I rarely treated myself to just-because purchases.

We said our goodbyes in the parking lot where we'd found side-by-side spots. I checked the time and phone for new texts. I'd sent Butcher messages to let her know I was okay every few hours since she left that morning. I thought I'd find it constraining to have someone who needed to know where you were, but it wasn't an abusive thing. She just wanted to know I was safe.

As I got in my car and closed and locked the doors, I sent her a text to let her know I was on my way home and asked if she knew what time she might get there. I put my phone away in my bag when I was driving. It had to be in my purse, and I wasn't to look at it. It wasn't a hard rule to follow. If I thought I'd be following orders from Butcher one day, I'd have called myself a liar.

She was just someone for my fantasies, but it was much better than I'd pictured since those dreams became reality. I was truly happy, and I hadn't thought anything was wrong with my life. You didn't know anything was missing until it arrived; Butcher was the final thing I'd been waiting on and hadn't known it.

19

BUTCHER

THE SCENTS OF MOTOR OIL, GAS, AND OLD GREASE HIT ME AS soon as I stepped into one of the bays of Darren's garage. Two of his workers checked me out as I approached the man's usual spot. He always used the one closest to the office since he wouldn't give in and hire some office help. I tapped the top of the hood and smiled as the man jerked his gaze to me. A smile instantly curved his mouth.

"Butcher, what are you doing here?"

"I wanted to talk to you."

He straightened and removed the red rag from the pocket of his coveralls. I was too aware of the other men staring at me. I already felt over-exposed. I'd practiced my speech a dozen times since I left work. How the hell did I do this, and why was I so nervous to talk to Darren? We'd become friends over the years.

"Everything okay with Toni?"

"She's perfect. You know that, and she doesn't know I'm here."

"You doing okay?"

"Yeah, well, you know I love your daughter, right?"

"If there's one thing I've always known, you're hopelessly devoted to that girl of mine."

"I know I got issues. That I'm always going to be an alcoholic and an addict, I may be clean and sober, but it's always there at the back of my mind. The cravings still hit me."

"Sobriety is a process, a daily choice, but you haven't slipped in two years."

"I want to marry her," I blurted out, and his smile got bigger.

"Is this you asking my blessing? Didn't take you for the old-fashioned type."

"This really isn't me, I don't ask anyone's permission for shit, but you've known me since I was a punk, broke college student. And that's why I needed to ask you. Your opinion is important to Toni…to me. I'll never feel good enough for her, but I love her more than anything in this fucking world. I can't promise I won't fuck up." I paused as I shoved my hands into my pockets, my left hand clenching around my sobriety coin. The edges cut into my fingers and palm. "And asking your blessing goes against everything I am, but I need it, man." I didn't realize how quiet it became until I stopped talking. I glanced around to find the other mechanics watching, almost frozen in place.

"Get back to work. I gotta talk to my future daughter-in-law," he announced as he motioned toward the office, but when I hesitated, he shook his head and went first.

I followed behind him, the weight lifted off my shoulders, but the anxiety lingered. Papers were piled up around an ancient desktop, and they shifted as he sat on the edge of his desk. He crossed his arms over his big, barrel chest.

"You know you didn't have to ask me. I was just waiting for the call to say she was engaged."

"I know I didn't, but I had to assure you that I'd take care of her."

He snorted and shook his head at me. "Butcher, you've done nothing but take care of her since she was sixteen. That hurt, that some asshole kid was my daughter's safe space for three years, and she didn't feel like she could come to me. And then you threatening me with those looks of yours, I felt like such a shit dad."

"That wasn't my intention, but your wife…she hasn't made Toni's acceptance of herself easy. I'm glad you came around, but if you hadn't, she was still mine to take care of. My girlfriend or not, she would've always been my babygirl."

"That was pretty clear when you told me before I left your apartment if I couldn't act right, I didn't need to come back."

I shrugged. "I had more balls than brains back then, probably still do."

"I'm not a fan of your job, but you're good at it. Charlie tells me enough that his business will go under if he ever loses you. You're sober and committed to staying that way. Most importantly, you have no shame in telling and showing everyone how much you love Toni. I always worried about her finding someone."

"Why?"

"Because they'd have to compete with you."

"I'm not much of a prize—asshole, remember?"

"But not to her. So if you want to marry her, just tell me when and where, but no eloping. I would like to walk my daughter down the aisle. It's a right dads have."

"That would be up to Toni, but eloping sounds like—"

"Don't even think about it. When are you asking her?"

"This weekend, she has this bed and breakfast in this cutesy little town she's been wanting to go to. I arranged to have the weekend off, but I pulled three days of all-nighters. I barely made it home before she went to work, which isn't unusual, so she hasn't gotten suspicious yet. When I pack her into the vehicle on Friday night, she'll be asking me questions. You think she'll say yes? I mean, six months is kinda quick for a proposal, right?"

He rolled his eyes at me. "You do know that most people think you've been a couple for years?"

"I've heard it a time or two." I smirked as he laughed. "Harry thought for the longest time we were already married until he got pissed at me one night when I hooked up with some woman at a bar we went to. I thought he was gonna take my head off for being disrespectful."

"I can see him doing that."

"Okay, I gotta get back to work. I got a guy I need to hunt down before I go home. He's a regular."

"Dangerous?"

"No, his lawyer doesn't think he's gonna show for his court date. He wants him to have a little reminder."

"You hired muscle now?"

"I think that's my main job description."

"Be safe, and you won't need it, but good luck this weekend."

"Thanks. I'll take good care of her, I promise."

"You always have."

I said my goodbyes and walked out of the office to see the guys still paying attention to us. I didn't bother saying anything as I headed for my truck. Only two more days, and I could take Toni away. We'd have the weekend all to ourselves. Even though I was sure she'd say yes when I asked her, there was a part of my brain that said it wasn't a guarantee.

My opinion on marriage was low at best, and I hadn't made any secret about it. She wanted to get married and maybe have kids. It was always a dream of hers. I didn't know if I was parent material. I barely kept myself alive most days. First, I needed to get her to agree to marry me. We'd work out the other details later.

I hopped up in the driver's seat and sent off a text to Charlie to let him know I was on my way to take care of my assignment. He just told me to call him when it was over. I put everything else out of my head, focused on the task at hand. My days of putting my safety last were in the past. Toni needed me to come home. I'd come a long way over the past two years. I don't think I wanted to die, but part of me knew that those three years of being drunk and high had made me careless.

My babygirl was my everything. Staying clean and alive was for her. I'd never be *fixed*. I did everything with my girl in mind. She was my anchor; I'd lost that for a while. In the process, I'd hurt Toni without intending to. I'd spend the rest of my life making up for it no matter what I had to do.

20

TONI

BUTCHER WAS BEING SECRETIVE. I GLARED AT HER FROM THE passenger seat. She'd met me at the door with a bag packed for both of us. Three hours into the drive, I'd started resorting to *are we there yet?* She just rolled her eyes and told me to relax, and we'd be there soon. I wanted to know where there was, and at almost hour four, a sign on the highway made my heartbeat increase.

I'd mentioned the Brandywine Harbor B&B several times; I'd even gone online to book a room but going alone didn't appeal. It was a small quirky blip on the map, an old artist collective they'd turned into a town. It wasn't Butcher's scene, but I should've known she'd remember, yet it shocked me she'd subject herself to playing tourist.

"You remembered?"

"Of course, I did." She reached across the console and placed her hand on my thigh, squeezed gently as she glanced at me. I saw her smile in the headlights before she turned forward again. "I worked almost doubles to get some of the names off the board so we'd have an entire weekend away. No one to show up unexpectedly. Two nights and two days of no phone, just you and sightseeing."

"But you hate things like this."

"But you love it, and I love you, and I know you'd never plan this trip alone. And you haven't had time away in forever, not since I took you to Greece for your birthday three years ago."

I remembered that trip. She'd handed me an envelope with the tickets. It was the only time in those three years of active addiction she'd stayed sober. I'd felt like I'd had my best friend back again, only to have her spiral when we returned home.

"Thank you." I rested my head back to take in her profile as it appeared in light and shadow. "And I love you, too." She gave me another gentle squeeze.

"I was going to wait until the morning, but this way, we get there tonight, then have all day to do whatever."

"We could've done something we both like."

"Stop, it'll be great, and you know I love making you happy, babygirl. I want to make sure that you have everything you need or want."

"You do, I know you stress over not giving me enough of your time, but it's not like I didn't know before I had to share you with Charlie and the guys."

She removed her hand from my thigh to signal and take the exit ramp. We drove a series of back roads until the town limit sign appeared in the headlights. I sat up a little straighter as I took in the darkened town. It was already close to midnight.

"Was it a problem us arriving this late?"

"No, Jane said she would be up. She had guests that left today and would be preparing rooms for three other couples arriving tomorrow. I called and double-checked before you got home. She said she was just off Main Street."

She slowed down to check the street signs and pulled off when she apparently saw the one she needed to turn on, and at the end of the street, asphalt turned to a gravel drive. We took the slight incline, and lights were on in a sprawling Victorian.

"It's prettier than the picture." I was excited to see inside. She pulled into a small parking area and told me to sit tight, and she'd come around.

I didn't know why she told me. I already knew she'd open my door, unbuckle me, and then help me out. I always joked about her gentlemanly ways, but I'd never met someone who still did the opening of doors. If we walked down a sidewalk, she always walked on the outside, shielding me from the street. Some people would consider it stifling, but I loved every second of the way she cared for me.

Before she helped me out, she grabbed our bag, and quickly we made our way inside. Her fingers securely laced through mine.

"You must be Aisling and Toni. I'm Jane." A slight woman with steel-colored hair appeared.

"Yes, ma'am, this is my girl, Toni." She brought our joined hands to her mouth to kiss the back of mine.

"It's a pleasure to meet you both. You made good time. Let's get you checked in. Everything you ordered arrived today and is in the room like you specified."

Jane turned to make her way to a reception desk tucked into a corner, and I shot a glance at Butcher, wanting to interrogate her on what she'd ordered. I only had to wait until we checked in, so I kept my mouth closed. I leaned against her as she filled out the paperwork, handed over her debit card and ID. The other woman kept watching us with a smile as I attached myself to Butcher, and she turned to brush her lips to my forehead.

"I'll get you into bed soon, babygirl." She took her card back, put it back in her wallet, and then shoved it into her back pocket.

"I'm fine."

"It's way past your bedtime." She slipped her arm around my waist as she bent to pick up our bag.

We followed Jane up the stairs to the second floor and she led us to a door at the end of the hall. "Here are your keys to your room and the front door." She handed me the keys. "I normally don't lock up until I go to bed around ten or so. If you need anything, don't hesitate to ask. I'll see you in the morning for breakfast around nine."

We told her thanks and goodnight, then Butcher released my hand and let me open the door. I walked inside and searched the wall for the light switch. As soon as I saw the bed, my breath hitched in my chest. Several vases of pink roses filled the room and in the center of the bed was a single box wrapped in hot pink paper.

I glanced over my shoulder to see her watching me, and I stumbled forward. My belly tightened as I heard our bag fall to the scarred hardwood floors, and the lock clicked into place. My fingers traced the delicate floral design on the cream-colored quilt.

"Go ahead. It's all yours." It was almost identical to the words she used sixteen years ago when I walked into her apartment. "Do you know, this was the same day I bought you your first dress?"

As I felt the first tear on my cheek, I didn't dare look at her. "It is?" My voice broke as I picked up the box, and it felt so tiny in my hands.

"Yep. Open it. I want to see what you think." The solid strength of her body pressed to mine from behind as her arms hugged my waist.

The white ribbon was almost garish against the bright pink. I pulled, and the bow gave easily. It floated down to the bed, settled and forgotten, as I removed the top of the square box to reveal the black velvet of the jewelry box inside. I nearly fumbled everything to join the ribbon. I swallowed around the lump in my throat as I eased the lid up, the hinge creaked, and then the tears fell. Atop a delicate rose gold band sat a medium-sized diamond.

"Butcher, it's beautiful."

"Toni." She said my name as she took hold of my hips and turned me until I faced her. "I know I'm no prize, and I can't make the important promises of sobriety and unlimited time with you, but I want this on your finger. I want everyone to know that you're taken, that your woman loves you more than anything in this world. I want you to have your perfect wedding, the dress I know you've dreamed of, and to have Darren walk you down the aisle. I need you to marry me, I know your logical brain is probably trying to say this is too quick, but this started sixteen years ago. At nineteen, I had no damn clue what it meant, but that first true smile, I needed to make sure it was always there. So, all you have to do is say yes, but if you want to wait, we can do that, too."

"Yes." I felt no hesitation. No fear of the unknown. Maybe she'd slip, but I also knew that she'd always come back to me. I held my breath as she took the ring box and removed the ring. I didn't miss that her hands shook as she slipped the band onto my ring finger.

I still wore my heels from work, and she cupped my face to bring my mouth down to hers. I moaned at the soft possessiveness of the kiss. Everything existed in the press of her lips to mine. All the love and a bit of fear. She held me close within her trembling arms.

"I love you, babygirl," she whispered as she broke the kiss.

"I love you, too. This really is the day you made your home my safe space?"

"Yes, I thought it was kinda nice to bring everything full circle. It's where it all started, even if neither of us knew it. Do you like it? Darren approved."

"Dad approved? He knew?"

"Yeah, well, I asked his permission first."

I snorted out a loud laugh and shook my head. "You don't ask anyone's permission."

"I told him the same thing, but he's known me. He knows how my addictions affected you. I wanted him to know that I would take care of you."

"He probably said you always took care of me."

She chuckled. "He did, but his opinion is important to you."

"Thank you."

"You're welcome and thank you for saying yes. I was a little nervous over that one. Now, let's get you ready for bed."

"Did you bring my—"

"Bonnet and all hair and skin products are in the bag. I brought you three outfits, and head wraps to match. How long have I been taking care of you? I know the important things." She tsked at me as she unzipped the back of my dress.

As the simple dress loosened, I let it slip from my shoulders. It fell but caught between our bodies. She took a step back to let it go the rest of the way to pool around my shoes. She undressed me like I was precious. Kissed me as if she couldn't resist just one more. She wanted and loved me, accepted me. She was the embodiment of my safe space.

She readied me for bed and tucked me in, and then she stripped away her clothes. I didn't let myself relax until she enveloped me in her arms. All the stress of the day disappeared because I knew I was loved. And as much as she was my comfort and safety, I was confident that I was hers, too.

EPILOGUE
BUTCHER

A Year Later

DID PEOPLE GETTING MARRIED TYPICALLY FEEL LIKE THEY were going to puke at any moment?

Toni wanted to get married on the day I proposed because she said it was an important date. It immortalized our milestones. No matter how much time passed, she still always got what she needed from me. People talked about going above and beyond, but that made it seem like there was a limit to your love and care. There was no limit when it came to my babygirl.

I jerked my head up as a knock sounded at the door. We'd come back to the bed and breakfast, rented it out for the wedding and honeymoon. We had a trip planned for later when we could both take two weeks off. I told whoever was knocking to come in, and I smiled as I saw my Dad and Darren.

"Hey, please say she's here?"

"She didn't make a run for it," Darren answered with a smile. He'd arrived without his soon-to-be ex-wife. We'd expected it, but it still hurt Toni's feelings her mother wouldn't at least attend the ceremony.

"You're not looking so good, kid." My dad approached and straightened my tie, and I tugged at the bottom of my bright blue vest.

"Were you nervous when you got married?"

"I still had my head in the toilet up until five minutes before I had to be at the altar. Your mother told me not to breathe on her during the ceremony. She barely wanted to kiss me, and I'd brushed my teeth. It was bad."

"Okay, I don't feel so bad now. At least I haven't puked yet."

"But I also had a stripper grinding on my lap until four a.m., and I was still slightly drunk when I got to the church."

"No stripper was grinding on me, and if I did it would've been the male variety. Since most of my groomsmen are gay and I told them to plan a party for them."

Charlie and Harry had taken care of planning the bachelorette party, I guess you'd call it. I'd had a blast, and since I didn't want anyone but my babygirl touching me, I let them plan it at a strip club for them. We'd taken immense pleasure in Tim getting his first lap dance. I'd never seen the kid turn that red before. He took it in stride, though.

"How's my babygirl? She have everything she needs?"

"I think all her maids of honor are a little jealous that you planned a full breakfast, spa treatment, and several little gifts for her to open to prepare for her to get ready." Darren shook his head.

"I think you might be cited in a divorce or two after today. At least that's what your mom said, and I wouldn't be surprised if a few husbands are gunning for you at the reception."

"Good, makes them have to step up their game."

"Carl, can I get a few minutes alone with Butcher?" Darren asked.

My dad nodded and kissed my cheek, telling me he'd be back to walk with me to where we'd set up in the backyard. Darren stayed silent until the door closed after my dad.

"A little late to say you disapprove."

"I don't disapprove. I wanted to give you this." He removed a flat box from his pocket and handed it to me.

When I opened it, I found a pocket watch. It was a bit worn and weathered with time.

"I gave Toni the necklace my mom gave Sue to wear. That was supposed to be handed down to the bride. My dad gave me that watch on my wedding day like his dad gave him. I wanted to carry on the tradition."

"Th—" I cleared my throat. "Thank you."

"No, Butcher, thank you. I have a beautiful and happy daughter because of you. You let her see the good in the world. Showed her she could have everything she ever wanted. And that was even before you were a couple. So one day, if you and she have those babies y'all talked about, you can pass the necklace and watch down. It's almost showtime. You look beautiful, Butcher."

He patted my cheek but didn't attempt to hug me, and I appreciated him respecting my personal space.

"She's beyond joyful that she's going to walk down the aisle to you. I've never seen a smile bigger in my life." He turned and left.

My dad returned, and I slipped the watch into the pocket on my vest, dad helped me on with my jacket, and we made our way outside to take our places. The minister gave me words of encouragement, and then the music started. I took three deep breaths and turned to look at Toni.

She wore a white headwrap with a tiny splash of pink rose buds pinned to it. Her dress was a simple white sundress that was so stark against her beautiful brown skin. It was almost the same style I'd bought her all those years ago. She was gorgeous inside and out, and she was all mine.

Who would've thought that I'd found the love of my life at nineteen?

Darren had her arm through his, but everyone else didn't exist except my woman slowly making her way toward me. I resisted the urge to grab her when she was close enough to touch. Darren kissed her cheek, and then she took the final two steps until I wrapped my hands around hers. They shook where they clasped the stems of her bouquet.

"Hello, beautiful," I whispered.

"Hey, handsome."

"You ready for this?"

"More than ready."

The minister cleared her throat, and we turned to look at her as she began the usual speech. I brought my attention back to Toni, stroked my thumbs over the back of her hands. I'd never believed in happily ever after. I definitely hadn't thought to earn this woman's love, but I'd spend the rest of my life proving to her that she'd always been meant to my babygirl and my life.

ABOUT THE AUTHOR

Siobhan Smile is an author of happily ever afters with a twist. They features characters of all sizes, shapes, sexualities, gender identities, and races. Reading a Siobhan Smile book lets you escape for a few hours whether that is to an alien world or a contemporary setting, you'll find something outside the norm. Writing books for Siobhan is more than simply telling a story, it's a way for everyone to see themselves get a HEA.

Author Pronouns: Nonbinary/Gender Nonconforming - They/Them

ALSO BY SIOBHAN SMILE

Little Love

His to Own, Hers to Claim

Shug's Daddy

Butcher's Babygirl

WRITING AS J.M. DABNEY

Sappho's Kiss Series

When All Else Fails

More Than What They See

Dysfunction it its Finest Series

Club Revenge

Soul Collector Prophecy

Twirled World Ink Series

Berzerker

Trouble

Scary

Lucky

Brawlers Series

Crave

Psycho

Bull

Hunter

Executioners Series

Ghost

Joker

King

Sin & Saint

Trenton Security

Livingston

Little

Gage

Pure

Masiello Brothers

The Taming of Violet

3 Moments Trilogy

A Matter of Time

The Men of Canter Handyman

Black Leather & Knuckle Tattoos

Chance at the Impossible

Bloody Knuckles Bar & Grill

Clipping the Gargoyle's Wings

New West City Universe

Co-written with Davidson King

The Hunt

Standalone

By Way of Pain (Criminal Delights - Assassins)

Christmas, Bloody Christmas (By Way of Pain Xmas Story)

Waited So Long

An Odd, Little Girl

Cold Cases and Second Chances

Claiming Whisper

A Yuri Sorenson Mystery

Not Another Statistic

Cold Cases Unit Series

Cold Cases and Second Chances

Cold Cases and Dark Secrets

Permanent Freebies

Has the Honeymoon Ended? (Brawlers Short Valentine's Story)

Once Upon a Bear Claw

The Scars She Bears (Executioners Short)